The Frolicking

GIRLS TRIP EDITION

GRANT WAMACK

BROKEN RIVER BOOKS

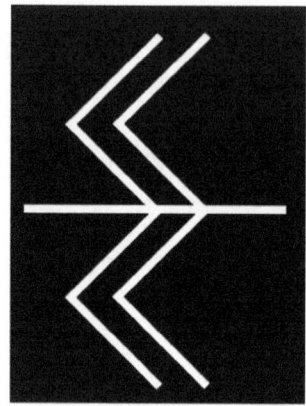

A Broken River Books Original
BROKEN RIVER BOOKS
Oklahoma City, OK
Copyright ©2024 Grant Wamack

Cover art by Don Noble
https://roosterrepublicpress.com/covers/
Interior layout design by Kelby Losack
https://kelbylosack.com/

ISBN: 978-1-940885-69-8

Printed in the U.S.A.

Praise for The Frolicking

"Fast, vivid, and intense! *The Frolicking* had me hooked from the beginning with its luminous prose, fascinating characters, and dialogue that rings with authenticity. This is one you do not want to miss!" — Brian Bowyer, Splatterpunk Award-nominated and Godless Award-winning author of *Old Too Soon* and *Metro Kinetic*

"A very entertaining psychedelic horror romp. If *Night of the Lepus* made you think rabbits couldn't be terrifying, this colorfully demented headtrip from Grant Wamack will change your mind." — Ben Arzate, author of *Elaine*

Contents

Dedicated to JDO

"Do not abandon yourselves to despair. We are the Easter people and hallelujah is our song." — Pope John Paul II

"It is far better to have frolicked, fell, and looked a fool than to never have frolicked at all." — Robert John Meehan

The Frolicking

GIRLS TRIP EDITION

GRANT WAMACK

BROKEN RIVER BOOKS

1

The Invitation

ELYSE DONABEDIAN SECOND-GUESSED HER vet school dreams behind a computer screen, cute bunny cursor hopping across a blank Word document. The past three years since declaring her major in wildlife biology were now riding on this essay. Elyse was beginning to doubt her decision.

Her love for animals went all the way back to childhood. She'd always possessed an almost supernatural empathy for anything furry that carried a pulse. She'd also always been squeamish at the sight of blood. The mere thought of a blood-stained manicure made her stomach queasy and sent her left eye to twitching. Despite these qualms, Elyse still held a deep desire to help animals, which far outweighed her fears.

She rolled her ergonomic chair back, plastic wheels sliding on plush carpet, and she took the pair of bulky pink headphones off her pierced ears. Her green eyes darted around the room in search of Yon Yon. She let the fat Harlequin bunny roam freely whenever she was home and could keep a maternal eye on him, but he enjoyed spending most of his time hopping around the elaborate enclosure she had built just for him.

It was a two-story wooden bungalow with a cute set of stairs, and an opening on the bottom floor with a beige cushion. A brown teepee sat adjacent to the home sporting a large bed inside and the chewed remains of spinach leaves scattered across the surface. Organic chew toys were strewn about the hay-filled landscape: a carrot here, a heart-shaped calendula, colorful loofahs, a timothy grass ball, and an apple wood molar string hanging from the second floor, ominously swaying side to side.

"Yon Yon, oh Yon Yon," she sang. "Where's my big butt Yon Yon at? Hiding in your castle again?"

Yon Yon sat in the corner of his majestic enclosure, cheeks jam-packed with alfalfa hay and orchard grass. He pooped out small round brown balls and continued chewing, staring into Elyse's eyes.

"You're the cutest thing ever, aren't you, Yon Yon? Yes, you are. Come here," Elyse said in a sing-song voice, stretching her arms out, tickling the air as Yon Yon came hopping over. "What would I ever do without you?"

Elyse bent down and gently stroked the top of Yon Yon's sloped furry head. She almost cried admiring the soft patches of black and white fur. They'd been together only two years, but she swore their bond went back much further than that, stretching beyond this dorm room and the confines of space and time. Perhaps they were companions in a previous incarnation, somewhere lovely like France, best buds frolicking through endless fields of long swaying grass and heralded by blue skies.

"Back to work I go," Elyse kissed him on the head. "Momma's gotta get her degree so she can help the rest of the animal kingdom live good lives."

Yon Yon continued chewing a mouthful of hay, content at the moment.

Elyse plopped back down on her chair, and considered ordering Yon Yon more snacks, but she knew it would be overkill. He was spoiled and she had to get back to work soon. Academic deadlines were nearing. She blew air through her nostrils and her curtain bangs fluttered forward and returned to rest on her large forehead. She clicked off the essay and scoured through Reddit, cooing at pictures of adorable bunnies with their owners. Her eyes lit up and her breathing grew shallow when she stumbled across a random post advertising an Easter-themed event.

DO YOU LOVE EASTER? COME TO MY SPECIAL EVENT—THE FROLICKING—THIS

SATURDAY. ONE DAY ONLY. FREE ALCOHOLIC BEVERAGES WILL BE PROVIDED WITH A TICKET. EASTER EGG HUNT, FRIENDSHIP, FOLLY, AND MORE!

Elyse clicked on the post and grinned as she scanned the contents written on a cute yet garish graphic. This felt like something she was destined to attend; pure joy flooded her being.

This is it! I have to go!

Elyse was stressed about her lack of Easter-themed activities planned for her favorite holiday, had been for two and a half months straight. Her parents booked a vacation to Fiji and wouldn't physically be present so spending time with her immediate family was out of the question. Locations she frequented in the past were too far or shut down thanks to the recession, causing her to almost pull strands of her wavy hair out with the sheer amount of stress on her shoulders.

This was it. This was a gift sent down by God. There was no other explanation. She just had to figure out how far Plainfield, Illinois was from the college campus and convince her roommates to come along. It seemed like an easy enough task.

Roommate #1: Brandi

Elyse knocked on Brandi's door, barely able to contain her excitement about the girls' trip she was planning.

No answer.

She sharply knocked again.

No answer.

Perhaps Brandi was deep in study mode with headphones on, texting some dumb guy, or lost in her own synth-heavy world. Either way, Brandi was going to hear her message. This was *vital,* and she had to let her closest friends know about the upcoming event. Nothing came above Easter, not even school. Elyse readied her fist and tilted her wrist back, pausing to inspect the pristine condition of her nude-pink nails with gold-outlined purple hearts.

Brandi opened the door, brown eyes transfixed to Elyse's fist hovering in the air. Lavish locs snugged up in a yellow hair tie, dimples peeking out the corner of an awkward smile. She wore red pajama pants and a white Fashion Nova Chinese Takeout crop top with the words THANK YOU ENJOY in bold red letters hovering above her flat brown stomach.

"Elyse, what's up?"

"Uh, sorry, I just wanted to make sure you heard me," Elyse put her fist down. "You busy?"

Elyse slid into the cramped room and inhaled the scent of shea butter wafting off Brandi as she looked at the towering stack of books and notes strewn across the bed. K-Pop softly spilled out a small speaker next to Brandi's open computer.

"I would have to say yes," Brandi said, gesturing to the same books that had Elyse feeling bad for intruding on the study session. "The grind never stops."

"Engineering stuff?"

"Yeah. A whole lotta engineering stuff and architecture. I don't know what possessed me to take that as an elective. It's giving me a major headache. At least the professor's cute."

"Can I have five minutes?"

Brandi softened her disposition and blew air out of her nostrils. Elyse and Brandi had been friends since high school. When Elyse's family moved from Glendale, California to Naperville, Illinois, she had a difficult time adjusting to the new town. She had grown accustomed to palm trees, big dinners, and weddings with distant family members.

Suburban and bland were the first two words that immediately came to mind every time she talked to her old friends who resided on the West Coast about her new home. Naperville was full of preppy kids and posers.

For whatever reason, Brandi had embraced Elyse, despite the two having distinctly different backgrounds. Brandi attended private school for the vast majority of her childhood, only recently transitioning to public school. Still, Brandi's smile always made her feel welcome, at ease, and *safe* in her new environment.

"I'm giving you three and a half." Brandi looked down at her phone. "Starting now."

"So, there's this Easter-themed event," Elyse looked at Brandi, struggling to gauge her friend's reaction.

"Go on…"

"It's in Plainfield. I've never been, but it sounds exciting. Like there'll be an Easter egg hunt, a maze, food, prizes, cotton candy, alcohol, and more. Said something about a brand-new world in the description."

"Plainfield is nothing but cornfields and white people. The furthest thing from a brand-new world. I'm sure you're not missing out on much of anything."

"Yeah, but it's an adults-only event. I think it'll be uber fun."

"I have so much schoolwork to do and exams to study for, Elyse. Unfortunately, I don't think I can make it."

"C'mon Brandi, you know how much I love Easter, pretty please," Elyse batted her eyelashes at her friend, knowing this manipulative tactic worked in the past like a charm.

"I'm sorry, but I just get bad a feeling about this. I mean we're celebrating a dead man coming back to life that we still don't even know existed, and not to mention veiled paganism. I support my witchy bitches, but I'm not one to ignore my intuition."

Elyse frowned. "Are you sure it isn't the keto diet you're on that's making your stomach hurt?"

"Shut up, Elyse. My gut health is gucci. Plus, I know my body. There's something off about this. I'm telling you…"

"Okay, but, hear me out."

"I feel like you're not in tune with your intuition. Maybe you should go to yoga class with Karmina, might help you become more grounded in your body."

"I'll think about it, but please reconsider, Brandi. It's just one night with the girlies."

"You pretty much told me everything there is to know," Brandi shifted her weight from her left foot to her right. "Where did you find out about this?"

"Reddit."

Brandi scoffed.

"C'mon, Brandi, do it for me," Elyse clasped her hands together in a faux prayer. "Do it for your friend."

"You're on the borderlands of emotional manipulation and I'm not going for it. No means no and that's that. I can do something on campus if you want, but I'm not going to this *thing*. For all we know, it's a bunch of furries pissing in bunny suits who smell like spoiled cabbage."

"Eww, Brandi."

"See, you never know. I'm just saying, people do weird things in the middle of nowhere, especially when they're bored." Brandi leaned over and squeezed Elyse's shoulder. "And Plainfield is the definition of boring. Think about the name—*Plain. Field.*"

"Okay, okay," Elyse threw her hands up in surrender. "I'll respect your boundaries, but my door remains open if you change your mind."

"Thanks, but this door is coming to a close," Brandi slowly closed the door, but not before blowing Elyse an air kiss. "Love you."

Roommate #2: Victoria

Victoria Doyle pushed her boobs together, wondering if it made her C cups look any bigger. Scoffing at her breasts in the mirror, she tossed aside another bra. She cursed her parents and her genetic makeup for not blessing her with bigger assets. Sure, she was conventionally attractive with long blonde hair, blue eyes, an athletic frame and a splash of freckles, but she wasn't Elyse pretty. Elyse had shimmering brown hair hanging down to her neck, strong cheekbones, perfect lips, and these green eyes that made the smartest men go stupid with lust. She yearned for that type of power, that type of control.

Someone knocked at the door softly, but with enough force that she knew exactly who it was. Victoria threw on an oversized t-shirt with Kobe on it. The shirt hung down past her ass she'd been working hard to grow in the gym the last few months. Glute-heavy workouts she copied from a variety of respected fitness influencers off social media. The vintage shirt belonged to this cute guy on the football team who'd continuously pursued her since sophomore year and to whom she'd finally given up the goodies. She pinched the fabric in between her index and thumb, smelling the pheromones and cologne-faded shirt.

A little funky, but it'll do. Just have to keep my distance and she'll never know.

She walked to the door, smoothed the wrinkles from her shirt, took a deep breath, and put on the biggest smile she could muster. An imaginary director in her head shouted *"rolling!"* and she eased into character, sliding on a well-worn mask—sweet roommate, great friend.

Got it.

"Speak of the angel herself, Elyse," she leaned on the door, trying her best to look inviting yet chill.

"I wouldn't say I'm an angel, but thanks, I guess," Elyse said, half-way smiling.

"What's up?" Victoria inspected Elyse, who had no makeup on whatsoever, but her skin still seemed radiant and flawless. *What skincare is this bitch using? Might have to steal some while she's sleeping.*

"So, get this… there's the cool Easter-themed event happening this weekend. I feel like me, you, and Karmina need to go. Just the three of us."

"What about Brandi? You didn't invite her?" A small glimmer of glee danced inside Victoria's stomach. Maybe she could stir the pot and get underneath Elyse's skin. She lived for drama and her instigation skills were elite.

"I talked to her already, but she declined my invite. You know how she is. Dedicated to her studies."

"Tell me about it," Victoria didn't know what the bitch was talking about but rolled her eyes as if on cue.

"Anyway, what do you think? Sounds like a lotta fun right?"

"This isn't going to have a bunch of screaming babies and soccer moms, is it? I don't like kids. They give me the ick."

"No, this is adults only. That's why I felt like you might be down. And I'm sure they'll be some cute guys in the mix."

"Cute guys? You don't say," Victoria unintentionally bit her bottom lip thinking about the possibilities. "There'll probably be liquor too."

"I mean adults do drink liquor," Elyse laughed, twirling her hair in her finger. "And it's free."

Victoria's right eye twitched and she wanted to smack the cute look off her friend's face. It took everything in her to keep her composure and look interested.

"Okay, I'm in."

"Yayyyyyy," Elyse said, jumping up and down. She squeezed Victoria in a bear hug.

Damn, Elyse smells good, Victoria thought, inhaling the fog of tuberose and rangoon creeper emanating from her roommate's pores.

The perfume calmed Victoria. She eased into the hug, enjoying the warmth and comfort, forgetting about her own body odor.

"You can let go now," Elyse said, slowly growing tense.

Victoria didn't realize how long they'd been entangled in each other's arms and she stepped back, embarrassed. Her mom didn't give her many hugs growing up and the men she slept with just wanted sex, looking at her body as an object. Starved of affection and intimacy, she felt out of sorts, but forced herself back into character.

"I'm uber excited," Victoria said. "Do we need to wear Easter-themed outfits?"

"No, there's no special clothing restrictions or anything like that. Wear what you want. I'm sure you'll choose something sexy."

"You know me too well. Sexy is my middle name."

2

The Eighth Limb of Yoga

"Hey girl, you must be bringing sexy back," a jock catcalled Karmina as she walked past the campus library, books tucked close to her chest, and the weight of her backpack slowing her down. She ignored the group of guys trying to get her attention, feeling their eyes groping her tan figure.

"Hey, I know you hear me talking to you, you dumb bitch." A man with curly hair and a patch of peach fuzz on his chin gripped her shoulder and she turned around. Pain throbbed through the muscle, and she wanted to smack the taste out of his mouth.

"Leave her alone," Elyse commanded. "And go bother someone else before I report you for sexual harassment, you dumb fuck."

"We don't want any smoke," the guy threw his hands up in the air and waved his entourage down as he continued down the hallway.

Karmina was dumbfounded. Elyse was cheerful and upbeat. She rarely heard the girl cuss and seemed like she never got in a fight in her life. Still, she stuck her neck out for her like a true friend.

"I appreciate that," Karmina said. "I didn't want to start a scene, but my blood was beginning to boil, and I knew my tongue was about to get me in trouble."

"It's okay," Elyse said. "I know you would do the same for me."

Karmina liked to think that she would do the same for her friend but wasn't quite sure. She was still trying to figure out life and she still didn't fully understand herself. Working out and becoming a gym girl was a new role she occupied and made her feel confident. If she could continuously overcome the stress and resistance of her body along with taming the animal parts of herself, she could do anything.

"So... we're still on for the yoga session?" Elyse asked.

"Oh yeah, for sure."

The two girls drove to a luxury gym where Karmina taught yoga classes and Pilates from time to time for extra income. It was good for her resume, helped her stand out, and kept her busy. Karmina pulled out her keys, slid it into the lock and let Elyse into the empty yoga studio.

It was an empty time slot between classes so they would have the room all to themselves.

Karmina lit some incense and put on a soothing zen music playlist curated by the rotating roster of yoga instructors. The abundance of plants, warm colors, and low lighting helped both of them relax even more.

"How have you been?" Karmina asked.

"It's been a stressful week with the class workload and looming deadlines, but I'm dealing."

"I feel you on the dealing part," Karmina said, stretching her toned arms behind her head. "Yoga is the perfect remedy for all your problems though."

"I'll namaste my way through it."

Both girls laughed.

"I love your laugh, it's so free and open," Karmina said.

"Thank you. I like your laugh too. I don't know why you see a problem with your own?"

"People can be assholes. You know how people like to judge you for the smallest things and my brothers used to pick on me growing up. Sorry for the trauma dump."

"No worries," Elyse attempted to follow Karmina's movements, joining in the much-needed stretch. "We all have trauma, it's almost a way of life, but how long will you let the shadow of your brothers haunt you and what does it matter?"

"Hmmm… maybe you're right. Note to self, stop being so self-conscious and laugh more."

"And I thought you were the teacher here."

Karmina playfully shoved Elyse off her yoga mat. "Okay, let's get down to business and follow my lead. Karmina led Elyse through several basic yoga poses, breathing slowly through her nose and exhaling through her mouth.

"Move into deer pose... yeah, just like that. Push into the earth back into downward facing dog and stretch out your legs."

"Like this?" Elyse leaned her back, rump in the air, a dull pain blooming in her shaky wrists.

"Yeah, don't forget to breathe."

"It hurts."

"Where?"

"My wrists and my lower back."

"Breathe into those spaces, breathe into the pain, and visualize the pain melting away."

Elyse nodded, took a deep inhale through her nose, and held the pose for a moment. Breathing into her wrists, she noticed the pain dissipating. Felt like magic.

"There's something to this yoga stuff."

"Stick with it and you'll experience great benefits over time."

The dim mood lighting flickered a fiery orange, throwing strange shadows across the wall. Karmina's breath hitched in her throat, a dry lump that wouldn't go away no matter how much she visualized it going down.

She slowly looked to her left, neck stiff with tension, the mat underneath her feeling like a rough sponge, hungry for her fear. Elyse disappeared and reappeared and disappeared again, a disorienting magic act if she ever saw one. Her friend's body stretched into startling shapes, arches and twists that didn't make sense to Karmina. She wished she could reach out and grab her friend's hand and yank it *hard* so she could have some sense of solidarity, some sense of control.

The lights returned to normal and both girls looked at one another, stunned by the technological anomaly that just occurred.

"What. The. Fuck," Karmina said.

"I couldn't say it any better myself," Elyse said.

"I think yoga is officially cancelled."

"You're the instructor. I'm not going against your word."

They hugged one another, Karmina secretly feeling the muscles in Elyse's back, making sure this was her friend and not the monstrosity she witnessed in the intervals of light and darkness. She slowly released a deep breath and the lights went out a second time, submerging both girls in an obsidian darkness.

They held onto each other for dear life.

3

Red Wings

E LYSE PULLED OUT A brown box and used her keys to cut the tape, which enclosed a purple vinyl player. She coughed as she opened the box and was assaulted by a strange plastic smell, one that was both familiar and disturbing.

"O-M-G," she said dropping her keys and covering her face with her hands. Her heart raced and she snatched her phone off the bed. She pulled up her contacts and called her boyfriend Skylar Osborne. "What's up, lovebug?" Skylar's firm voice answered, giving Elyse a wave of relaxation and security.

"Babe, I need you to come over ASAP. It's an emergency."

"Oh god, what happened? Are you okay?"

"Styrofoam crisis."

"I'm at the gym, lovebug. I'm getting gains. Can't one of your roommates help you?"

"They're out doing school stuff. I'm solo dolo right now. I *really* need you, Skylar. You know how I get when it comes to Styrofoam. Gives me the absolute creeps and I'm highly sensitive to that sound."

Skylar sighed and the sound of weights clinked in the background. "I'm finishing this set of squats and then I'll be right over. Close the box and watch TV or something in the meantime. We don't need you having a panic attack."

"Thanks, babe. You have no idea how much this means to me. I love you."

"Love you too."

Click.

Skylar pulled up in his black Nissan Altima blasting Travis Scott's *Utopia* album. Elyse's windows facing westward rattled from the bass erupting out of her boyfriend's speakers. She thought it was cute the first six times she heard the album, but now she wondered if something was wrong with her boyfriend. The album was so dark and discordant. Elyse couldn't handle the sonic rhythms. She preferred bubblegum pop, r&b, songs about love.

Elyse buzzed him upstairs and cracked the door open for him. A few minutes later, he came running up the steps like a rhino. Each footstep heavy as a sledgehammer.

Nothing about her boyfriend was quiet, his existence was loud and full of testosterone.

"Lovebug, I'm home."

Elyse hugged him tightly, relishing the comfort and safety of thick muscular arms and a sizeable upper body. Even though he was sweaty, she was able to breathe easier, taking in the scent of his pheromones. He ran his tatted hands through his curly brown hair, inked skeleton bones poking through his locks.

"How was your workout?"

"Decent. Where's the Styrofoam?"

"Right under your nose, meathead."

"Don't call me a meathead. I read books too, y'know."

"I'm just kidding."

Skylar laughed, but Elyse could hear the pain underneath the gesture. He maintained a tough facade and busted his ass in the name of gains, but he was soft and tender with her. She wished he would just open up and tell her why he carried this weight on his shoulders. She would love him just the same even if he was skinny.

He stuffed the Styrofoam into a garbage bag while Elyse plugged her ears with her index fingers. She hated the sound of the dreadful material and wished companies would come up with a quieter shipping alternative.

Skylar took out the trash and wiped his hands dramatically as if he completed a task of mythic proportions.

"Thank you, babe. You're the best."

"I try."

Her boyfriend put on a Barry White record and pulled out a condom, waving it in the air like a trophy.

"Really babe?" Elyse put her hands on her hips.

"What, you want me to hit it raw?"

"No, you imbecile. I'm on my period."

"I don't care."

"I know you don't care, but I do."

Her boyfriend hung his head in defeat. "It's just a little blood. I mean you gave me my red wings."

"Don't remind me," she cringed, remembering the night from seven months ago, when they got too drunk off Buzz Balls. She was feeling adventurous and didn't think he would actually follow through with the dare.

Her boyfriend ate her out like a greedy dog, lapping her fluids mixed with her blood. His tongue darted in and out of her vagina, licking her inner walls clean. She shone her cellphone's light on his smiling face and blood covered the lower half like some sick Rorschach test gone wrong.

She shook away the disgusting memory and tried to anchor herself back into the current moment. Skylar pulled her in close and kissed her on the lips and the warmth helped her feel safe and secure. She grabbed his neck and kissed the tatted outline of her lips - red and sensual. Most people said this was the sign of a fuck boy, but Elyse dismissed these claims and knew it was a testament of love. What could be better than that?

"If you're lucky, I'll give you some when I get back home," Elyse smiled coyly. "I know I'll be in a great mood."

"Say less."

Elyse gave him another kiss, tasting salt and the remnants of pea protein powder coating his tongue. She didn't care, she wanted to taste every bit of his essence. His erection poked against her belly button, straining against his sweatpants.

"Are you sure you'll be safe out there?"

"Yeah, what's the worst that can happen?"

"I mean I trust you, but I don't trust other people. I looked up the post but couldn't find any more information on the event. No social media posts, no reels, no videos. Nothing. Don't you find that strange?"

"Not really. Feels exclusive. Like she doesn't want a lot of people coming."

"Yeah, that girl's profile picture gives me the creeps," Skylar's brow furrowed. "Her huge bunny chompers are weird. They look fake, almost like veneers."

Elyse shoved her boyfriend playfully. "Don't be mean. I think she looks cute. They're just teeth."

"What, you want to make out with her?" He laughed. "I'm not opposed to it."

Elyse crossed her arms. "Don't be like that."

"Okay, okay, but still… I want you to be safe, so I brought you a gift."

"It better not be a gun," Elyse said, bracing herself for the worst. "I hate those things. I'd be too scared to even pull the trigger."

"No, something even better." He rummaged in his backpack and fished out a large black can with a vicious-looking grizzly bear painted across the metal.

"Bear mace!" she almost shrieked. "You have to be kidding me."

"I kid you not."

"Isn't this illegal?"

"Who cares," he said. "At least you'll have something in your purse just in case some drunk idiot tries groping you or following you back to your car. I hate even thinking about the possibility."

"Well, I do appreciate your worry. It's kinda cute and endearing."

"I need my Armenian princess to come home in one piece," he smiled. "Promise you'll bring it."

"Okay, I promise I'll bring it," Elyse said gripping the bear mace and squeezing his left tricep with her free hand. "I don't know why everyone's so worried about this event."

"Who's everyone?" Skylar leaned in closer, waiting for the answer to spill out of Elyse's soft lips.

"Just you and Brandi."

"See, I'm not crazy."

"I never said you were crazy. You can be overly protective sometimes. I must be blind because I don't see the issue."

"I know that face and I know that stance. You're not budging, are you?"

"Nope. Not an inch."

"Okay, just keep your phone charged. I'll call you just to make sure you're alive."

"You two are being such worry warts. What's the worst that could happen? A tummy ache?"

"You never know…"

Elyse stared into the vicious eyes of the bear on the mace's logo. Something about the disposition disturbed her. The can rattled in her trembling hand as she placed it next to her keys on the nightstand.

4

Take a Shot for Me

THE EVENING SKY RESEMBLED runny eggs and lavender smeared across the horizon. Victoria sped down I-88, weaving in and out of traffic. She loved being in the driver's seat and didn't mind Elyse sitting next to her, eyes glued to her phone with plastic bunny ears fixed to the back and Karmina sprawled out in the backseat staring out the rear window. Something about being in the driver's seat made her feel in control and the rush of pavement rumbling underneath the tires made her feel alive. Following the car's navigation displayed on the center monitor, she took exit 121, headed towards Eola Rd., and then a sharp left onto US-30E. Cruising down several side streets, she felt accomplished as she sped by a blue and white sign proclaiming *Welcome to the Village of Plainfield*.

Finally, here.

Wind turbines dotted the flat landscape along with farmland, rotor blades slashing through the warm sky. The white sentinels moved silently as they churned the wind, creating lift and drag, moving in hushed circular patterns. The torpid movement was hypnotizing like the gloved hands of a mime, a dark performance signaling something deeper going on in the firmament. Victoria squeezed the steering wheel and swallowed hard, saliva coating her tonsils. She felt like the turbines were feeding on her attention, feasting on the anxiety thrumming through her tense neck, alchemizing her raw emotions into electricity.

A warm hand rested on her thigh and Elyse's soft voice snapped her attention back to the road. "You okay?"

"Y-yeah I'm good," Victoria wiped the beads of sweat on her forehead with her left hand, slightly shaken by the turbines receding into the background. "Thanks though."

Elyse didn't look like she believed her, but she smiled and turned back to her phone. Probably texting her muscle-head boyfriend, Victoria figured. She took a deep breath and a sip from the warm water bottle sitting next to her. It tasted off, but she brushed the negativity away and turned up the volume on the car's speakers, skipping past a viral Big Poliano freestyle and a Young Beezly single, finally settling on Doja Cat's "Paint the Town

Red." The girls yelled out the lyrics and bounced around their seats as the flat grassy landscape, home to 40,000 people, welcomed the three girls further into its emerald maw.

"Isn't it strange they call this a village? You ever think about that?" Karmina asked, playing with a strand of black hair, twisting it around her index finger. "Like a random group of friends and lovers take some horses and go out in the wild with no maps, no phone. Maybe some burlap sacks filled with their most treasured belongings and some rusty tools. They build huts, maybe a local store, a farmer's market, a church, just hoping they can start a community, praying they can build something that will last."

"I don't know if it's stupid or brave," Victoria said. "But it's giving dirty and exhausting."

"I think it's sweet, but like the term village does seem outdated," Elyse said. "Plainfield's growing crazy fast or at least that's what the internet says."

"It's probably all of these things, but it looks like it worked out for the best," Karmina said.

The best.

Something about this conversation gave Victoria the creeps. She'd driven through here with family and even shopped at some local stores and fashion boutiques, but it always seemed boring and small. Of course, there was a growing community like Elyse said, but the energy of

Plainfield seemed small and contained. Like the people weren't meant to extend past a certain size as if a psychic barrier had been erected long ago by a village chief. As if the village was always meant to remain a village, no matter how far civilization advanced.

"About fucking time," Karmina said, playfully kicking the back of Victoria's seat.

"Can you stop, please?" Victoria asked.

"Chill out," Karmina groaned. "I'm just fucking with you."

"Everyone, relax," Elyse commanded. "This is supposed to be a fun girl's night out and I don't want you ruining my favorite holiday."

"Favorite holiday," Victoria mumbled under her breath.

"What was that?" Elyse said, shooting emotional daggers out of her clear eyes. Something about the pointed expression made Victoria shrink into her seat. Usually, Elyse was all smiles and fluff, but Victoria knew she wasn't fucking around.

"Oh n-nothing. Just allergies messing with me."

"You need a tissue?" Elyse said, seeing through the lie, but accepting the admission of defeat.

"No, I'll be okay. Thank you though."

Victoria pulled up to the large parking lot, taking note of the lack of cars. Cracks ran through the asphalt like bulbous green veins, and thick vegetation threatened to take back the land. Wind rustled through the Norway Maple, American Elder, and Mulberry trees, arching the trunks downward. The wood creaked erotically, almost sounding like a feminine moan. Victoria shook it off, attributing the hallucinatory sound to her pent-up sexual desires. She thought back to her psychology class and wondered what Freud would say about this.

She looked at the massive cornfield which seemed to have been barren and untouched for years. Rows of piss yellow land sat next to fields of grass buffered by a couple of abandoned farm buildings and a small house. Two hundred yards out, stacks of hay could be seen, arranged in a strange pattern. Almost reminded her of a crop circle, but different.

"This is giving me a major ick, Elyse," Victoria said. "I thought I might be able to meet a cute boy or something. It's like no one got the memo about the event."

"I have to admit it's weird, but we drove out all this way," Elyse said, stretching her limbs and joints cracking loudly. "We need to at least check it out. Maybe there's another parking lot or people are running late. The night is still young."

The night is still young. Of course you would say that, stupid bitch.

"Alright, we're checking it for you Elyse, but if it's dry, we're dipping, okay?" Karmina said, looking around.

"Welcome to Plainfield, a bunch of cornfields and grass. Too much if you ask me. What a blast," Victoria said, spinning in a dramatic circle with her arms outstretched. She kicked a dead cornstalk.

Karmina moved in close to Victoria and pinched her arm.

Victoria yelped. "What the fuck, Karmina."

"Stop being a bitch," she whispered. "You know how much she loves Easter. The least we could do is pretend to be supportive. Shit."

"Okay, I'll chill," Victoria whispered back. "Just promise not to pinch me again."

"I promise."

"There's a sign," Elyse pointed.

The three girls turned their heads in tandem, looking at a sign shaped like an arrow sticking out of the grass, wood warped and soaked with dry rot, with the words "Easter Event-this way" painted in a fresh crimson red, fumes waded off the sign. Cicadas buzzed somewhere in the distance and the adjacent road remained empty.

The three girls followed the sign which led them to a shadowy booth, which dislodged a buried memory from the depths of Victoria's subconscious. A booth with an uncanny resemblance to the same one she remembered seeing at a Mexican circus that rolled through town when she was younger. She begged her religious parents to go and they caved, especially since they'd been arguing frequently and the first signs of an impending divorce were rearing its ugly head in her household. Her parents let her eat a hotdog, a funnel cake, guzzle down an orange soda, and she ate so much cotton candy she got nauseous, but the gluttonous experience was worth it or so she thought. Something about the memory made Victoria's stomach clench up, a hazy vision of someone staring at her from the booth with a perverse grin on his face and long jowls like a dog in heat. He had waved at her calling her "fatty." The comment trigged her, and she erupted in tears. Somehow her parents didn't hear the comment and thought she was lying, scolding her for the indiscretion. That moment left an emotional scar on her that never quite healed.

A figure stood behind the booth, a tall lanky man of sorts. He wore a blue jumpsuit similar to one a janitor would wear but this was worn, stained with all manner of liquid and paint splotches. Deep tears and scratches crisscrossed the poly/cotton fabric. The way the man stood was funny like he was missing part of his spine and lacked some vital bones, tendons, and muscles in his back. The silent type. He leaned precariously to the right. His shadowy face seemed cloudy and stretched underneath his baseball cap that said "Plainfield Pride" in blocky yellow letters with a cartoonish tractor under it.

"Must be a proud local," Victoria muttered under her breath sarcastically.

Elyse glared at Victoria.

"What?" Victoria said. "It's a valid observation."

Bottles of liquor were lined up behind the man who they assumed was a bartender. He stood there, super still, waiting for their order.

Elyse approached the booth first, taking cautious steps and looking around. "Hi sir, how are you doing today?" she noticed a bunny pendant pinned to his chest, shifting slightly as if something was moving inside his sternum. "I love your bunny pendant by the way."

"It's cute," Karmina chimed in.

The man said nothing.

"He's kind of a weirdo," Victoria whispered.

Karmina elbowed Victoria in the ribcage, and she swallowed the pain like an overly ripe pomegranate. Exhaling a sharp breath through her mouth. She hoped the blow didn't leave any bruises on her skin.

"What do you girls want to drink?" Elyse asked.

"It's feeling like a Tequila type of night," Karmina said, eyeing the bottles. "Let's get three shots of that Clase Azul Reposado in the back."

"Isn't that the expensive shit I see bottle girls with and clout chasers drinking all the time on social media?" Victoria asked. "If so, count me the fuck in."

"Yep," Karmina said, watching the bartender jerkily grab the blue and white bottle off a shelf behind him. He blew dust off the bottle and unscrewed the silver lid with a limp hand. "This *mamarracho* knows exactly what we need."

"As long as it's good and gets you girls to stop arguing, I don't care," Elyse said.

"It's smooth as hell," Karmina said. "Believe me, I won't care about a thing in the world after a couple shots of this."

The wheels got to turning inside Victoria's head. She wondered how Karmina knew this, her friend said this with such conviction as if she had drunk this tequila firsthand, as if she'd experienced it multiple times. She was pretty and fit and Venezuelan. A killer combo when it came to attracting the opposite sex. Maybe she had met someone at a nightclub, a professional ball player or even one of the Chicago Blackhawks. She wondered if the girl had a large jersey balled up in her closet with the musty scent of sex and pheromones coiled into the stretchy synthetic fibers.

"Why are you looking at me like that?" Karmina said, curling her lips. "Like you just swallowed an undercooked piece of steak or something."

"Oh nothing," Victoria said. "Just admiring your outfit."

Karmina seemed to accept the answer and Victoria knew she had to stop letting her true colors rise to the surface. She had to buckle down, sharpen her acting chops, and readjust her social mask. She didn't want anyone to ever see her for who she truly was.

"Bottom's up," Elyse said, grabbing a shot glass and passing the two others to Victoria and Karmina, instantly defusing the tension growing in the air.

They tossed the shots back and Victoria was surprised by how smooth it was despite a burning sensation worming its way down her chest. Made her feel warm and alive.

"That was great," Victoria said, surprised by the excitement in her voice.

"I know, right," Elyse chimed in.

"Told ya," Karmina said, eyeing Victoria when she said this statement. It was almost as if Karmina could see through her façade as if she was onto her.

Victoria shivered and attributed it to the wind whistling through the sparse trees. She leaned against the booth and the bartender let out a strange grunt as he staggered back, bumping into the shelf behind him. He collapsed and his oily face smushed inward and a tawny brown field mouse climbed out of his neck, sniffing the air, followed by another and another. His body fell to the ground and a mischief of mice escaped from the seams of his coveralls and underneath his ballcap. They streamed out of the booth, climbing on top of one another, disappearing into the grass as Elyse screamed and Victoria discovered a similar sound escaping her own throat. Karmina watched with a cold-faced stare and the bartender was no more.

"Am I hallucinating?" Victoria asked, breathing in a labored way like she just run sprints for a track meet. "Or were those rats that just ran out of the alcohol booth?"

"No, those definitely were rats," Karmina said.

"Field mice," Elyse corrected them both through heavy breaths. "They carry diseases and have sharp teeth. Hate it."

"Forgot you were the animal expert," Victoria said.

"I'm not fucking with diseases or sharp teeth," Karmina said, pulling out hand sanitizer out of her black Coach backpack with soft pebble leather and glove-tanned leather fabric lining. She sprayed her hands and passed it around to the other girls.

"Shit, almost gave me a heart attack," Elyse said, rubbing her hands together before feeling her chest.

Karmina looked into the booth and Victoria followed suit. The weathered coveralls were completely flat and a fleshy mask sat on top of the fabric. "Weird."

"Understatement," Victoria said, still not sure what to make of the display she just witnessed. Maybe this was a gag or part of the event, but it had nothing to do with Easter. She struggled to wrap her head around the spectacle and began feeling like she was a character in a lost chapter of *Alice in Wonderland.*

Before she could analyze the event any deeper, a pretty Japanese girl with a gap-toothed smile sauntered towards the girls with a shovel in her arm, the wooden pole taller than her 5'7" height. She leaned against the shovel's handle and politely curtsied, pulling on the hem of her black Prada Nylon overall skirt and a white tee covered the subtle curve of her shoulders. Tall black socks brought attention to the girl's discolored knees. Purple and wet with dirt.

What was this girl doing in the dirt? She's far too pretty to be doing manual labor.

"Hiiiiiiii, I'm so happy all of you could make it. Welcome to the Frolicking. I mean it hasn't happened quite yet, but we'll catch up first and let the sun dip beneath the horizon and allow Mother Moon to make an appearance."

"Mother Moon?" Karmina asked, confused by this girl.

"Yes, Mother Moon, she bathes us in her brilliant light. She helps guide us through our cycles. She nurtures us even when we sleep. I love her so much. Sometimes, I even give her a bouquet to show her my appreciation."

"Cool," Elyse said, always the one to be aware of a conversation on the brink of becoming derailed.

"I'm glad you girls are helping yourselves to some refreshments. Low turnout this year, unfortunately."

"Yeah, I was wondering where everyone was at," Victoria looked around the empty event. "Are we the only ones here?"

"In a sense, yes," the unnamed host said. "People seem so scared these days since COVID happened. It was years ago, but people are moving like they're stuck under an internal lockdown. Like rodents. Conditioning is my best guess. Where was I? Oh yeah, Reddit probably wasn't the best move. The platform is dying. My name's Stephanie by the way, Stephanie Kusama, but you can call me Steph. All my friends do."

"Cool meeting you Steph," Karmina extended her hand and cringed as Stephanie shook it, leaving dirt stains on her palm.

Stephanie wiped her dirty hands on her overalls and shook bits of soil from her black waterfall braid. Somehow her hair still shimmered like a shampoo commercial. Victoria wondered how the girl could afford such an expensive outfit and if she owned the farmland. She had to, considering how careless she was with the clothing's upkeep.

"What were you doing before you found us?" Elyse asked, curiosity getting the best of her. "Digging holes?"

"How'd you know?" Stephanie said. "Rabbit holes to be precise."

"Why?" Victoria asked. "That's kinda weird."

Stephanie's eye twitched and she blinked, moving into another space. "The rabbits hide things in their holes, valuables, think of things like occult knowledge, objects, pieces of the moon. The sneaky bastards know what's coming and it's up to me to get to the bottom of it. Do not listen to the rabbits, the rabbits are greedy and ravenous. Be careful who you trust."

"O-okay," Victoria said, glaring at Elyse and Karmina. They shrugged in response as if they didn't hear this nutcase riff about rabbit holes.

Stephanie's left eye twitched again and her facial muscles seemed to relax. "You have to excuse me, sometimes I can be a bit heady at times and forgetful. I'm going to wash up and change real quick for tonight's festivities. I hope you girls don't mind."

"No, not at all," Elyse said. "Take your time."

Stephanie curtsied once again, only this time there was something cute and disarming about it. So disarming, it almost made Victoria forget about what she said a moment earlier. The girl seemed all over the place mentally and Victoria had a hard time getting a handle on her. It made her feel uneasy and on edge. She watched Stephanie skip away into the distance, disappearing into the tall grass, swinging the shovel like a pendulum, slicing through the air.

"We should probably go," Karmina said.

"Yeah, I co-sign Karmina's statement," Victoria said, already picturing herself back in the driver's seat, leather under her butt and a steady hand on the steering wheel.

"Hold on," Elyse said. "Let's think about this."

"Hold on, hold on?" Victoria said. "That girl is touched in the head. There's nothing to think about."

"I mean you two are right, she is strange and maybe she is suffering from a mental illness, but that doesn't mean we should demonize her."

"We're just being real," Karmina said. "I know you're being nice and idealistic, but we don't know what this crazy girl is capable of."

"Neurodivergent, not crazy," Elyse said, putting her hands on her hips. Her sustainable beige tote bag hanging off her shoulder rippled in the wind.

"Okay, fine," Karmina said. "Neurodivergent."

"Plus, no one else is here." Victoria thought there might be a couple of cute guys, but there wasn't much of anything. Random buildings, farmland, tall grass, haystacks, and rabbit holes somewhere in the distance.

"We drove all this way and you guys know how much Easter means to me."

Victoria and Karmina looked at each other, knowing this was a losing battle and that Elyse somehow discovered the path to victory two steps ago.

"Okay, but if this Stephanie girl starts doing something wild, we're leaving with or without you," Karmina said.

Elyse excitedly hugged Karmina before giving Victoria a tight squeeze. Something about Elyse's hugs was always calming, warm, and genuine. Like a warm blanket and hot chocolate in the middle of a Midwest blizzard.

"I don't know about you, but I need another drink," Karmina suggested, moving back to the bar. She poured three shots of tequila.

They clinked their shot glasses.

"Let's cheers to something." Elyse suggested.

"Like what?" Victora said, anticipating the warmth.

"To sanity," Karmina said, laughing.

"And to Easter."

"To sanity and Easter," they all said in unison, downing the shots. The memory of the mice seemed like a figment of her imagination, a light receding deep into Victoria's psyche. She watched the last embers of the dimming sun get swallowed by the horizon and the sky above them darkened significantly.

5

The Sweet Nectar of the Unknown

S TEPHANIE RETURNED WITH A brown wicker basket lined with a white napkin, and a bottle of liquor with something serpentine swishing inside. She wore a stunning pink and gold brocade mini dress with an angled waistband and a tulle skirt. Dainty ribbon straps hung down her arms, exposing the curve of her shoulders and there wasn't a single speck of dirt in sight. Small flowers stuck out of her luxurious hair: wild bergamots, red columbines, cotton milkweed, and wild geraniums. You would have thought she was going to attend a fancy Easter ball with a pack of social media influencers and A-list celebs, but here she was in the middle of nowhere, ushering the girls toward some unknown destination in the most glamorous way possible.

"Phones, please," Stephanie said, extending the basket forward, a smile plastered across her pretty face. Her skin seemed to shimmer in the moonlight. "The Frolicking is special and cannot be recorded. We must be present and dive into the heart of *now*."

Karmina barely registered what the girl said, still somewhat enamored by the dress and the gap in her front tooth seemed to envelop her. The name of the liquor in Stephanie's hand was nagging at the back of Karmina's mind, tugging on a rolodex of spirits, but she couldn't remember it for the life of her. She shivered slightly, noticing a slight chill in the night air, but she was thankful for the tequila coursing through her body, keeping her core warm and toasty.

Elyse handed over her phone, not to anyone's surprise, acquiescing to Stephanie's demands. Karmina wondered if she had fallen victim to the girl's hypnotic aura and was being swayed by unknown forces. She couldn't blame her since she too felt like she'd follow this girl into a dark cave or jump off a cliff into the looming abyss if she suggested it.

"I can't," Victoria said, visibly flustered and annoyed.

"Why?" Stephanie asked, cocking her head to the side. Karmina watched her eyes, expecting one to twitch.

"I'm expecting some important texts," Victoria said, looking down at her phone like it was the holy grail, knuckles growing white from squeezing too hard.

"C'mon, Victoria, just give her the phone," Elyse said. "Let's live in the moment. It'll be liberating. I already feel better without that thing in my tote bag."

Hearing that statement triggered a memory in Karmina's head, a hazy flashback to a time she did shrooms in Venezuela. Golden teachers were the name of the strain from what she recalled. Something meant for beginners, a gateway. She just graduated high school and was staying with family for the summer before she would go away for college. It felt like a strange liminal space before entering true adulthood. A friend encouraged her to try shrooms, suggesting that it would prepare her for the unknown expanse ahead of her.

She found a secluded spot along the Orinoco River, settling down by a cluster of kapok trees that towered over her, 200 feet in height. Frogs croaked and colorful birds twittered inside the crooks of the massive trees surrounding her. The humidity made her tank top stick to her skin like a leech, sweat seeping through the fabric. Ignoring her discomfort and the swaying shadows, she carefully weighed the shrooms, making sure not to consume too much.

They tasted bitter and rancid, tongue coated in a malodorous residue. Karmina washed it down with bottled water, but the taste remained. Fifteen minutes passed and she could still taste the nastiness on her tastebuds--earthy and acerbic. Her body felt weird and the firm world around her seemed to loosen up while her flesh became weighted, almost sliding down the bone.

Karmina took deep breaths, leaning on her yoga practice to anchor back into a safe space. She stuffed her index fingers into her ears, softly pressing against the cartilage, inhaling through her nose and exhaling through her mouth, making a slight humming noise, reverberating through her throat, and traveling down her body. She instantly felt more relaxed and her nervous system calmed down. Despite this moment of comfort, she could still feel the shrooms digesting in her stomach, enzymes and juices breaking the hallucinogen down.

The insects crawling on the earth a couple of feet in front of her trailed a blue flame behind them before burrowing into the soil, and the trees began to breathe. Karmina heard *them* taking in carbon dioxide into their wooden lungs, and exhaling oxygen. Something about it sounded monstrous and menacing. She wondered if she had taken too large a dosage or if the shrooms were laced. Could shrooms even be laced?

Paranoia was beginning to get the best of her and her sense of time slipped out of her hands. Weird shapes zipped past her ears, whispering things to her in foreign languages, ancient tongues her mind insisted. Part of her could understand it on a physical level, her body translating the lingo into something inherently understandable, and this dark understanding made her sweat twice as hard.

She looked up at the trees, hoping the ligneous juggernauts would give her some sort of comfort, but they were silent. She could feel them purposely keeping words to themselves, the branches seemed so far away. The white and pink flowers embedded in the bark seemed to spit at her while a solitary bat fed on the sickly nectar spilling from the center of the plant blossoms, glands wet with sweet viscous secretions. The nectar smelled foul, curling through her nostrils, causing her stomach to clench. Bending over, she coughed up some shrooms in a yellowish puddle and this brought her some relief, glad to have gotten rid of some of the fungi. Maybe this would reduce the time she would be stuck in this space.

The bat dropped down, six wings attached to its back, and zoomed directly over Karmina's head. She ducked down, hands clenching her hair as if a bomb was about to detonate.

Grabbing her phone, she needed to know the time. Maybe that would give her some security, knowing that there was only so much time left. She jabbed in her pin code and couldn't read the screen on her phone, the apps shook violently and the numbers melted into a white mess. Tossing the useless device aside, she curled up into a ball and closed her eyes, remembering how these trees were used to build dugout canoes and coffins. Imagining one of these trees becoming her coffin almost made her hyperventilate. She crawled as far away from the trees as possible and stared at the sky until the shrooms began to wear off. On shaky legs, she gathered up her belongings and made her way home. The entire experience scared her off shrooms and hallucinogens permanently.

"What if your boyfriend calls you or you need the police for an emergency?" Victoria said. "Make it make sense."

She's making a good point for once.

"We're safe," Elyse said with puppy dog eyes, silently pleading with her friend. "There's nothing to worry about. We got each other."

"I'll take good care of your phones and I'll be sure to give them back when the night's over," Stephanie said, petting a phone. Her nose twitched and she moved closer to Elyse. "You have my word."

Elyse looked visibly uncomfortable, unsure as to what was happening. She took a step back. Karmina wasn't sure what was going on either, Elyse always smelled good and had great hygiene practices in place. Either way, she was prepared to defend her friend if Stephanie started getting touchy or went off the hinges.

"Is that what I think it is?" Stephanie asked, nostrils somehow opening wider, inhaling Elyse's scent. Sniffing. Snorting.

"A Reason to Love, my perfume?" Elyse asked, cautiously sniffing her own armpit. "I hope I don't smell bad. I swear I showered before coming here."

"No, even though the damask rose, agarwood, and peony notes are some of my favorites...you own a bunny."

"I do," Elyse looked astounded. "How'd you know?"

"Scents hold so many secrets, so much raw data about a person. I like discovering these secrets like an olfactory archaeologist. Let me go deeper."

Stephanie plucked two hairs off Elyse's shirt and brought them up to her nose, closing her eyes and deeply inhaling.

"The royal jester of rabbits, the Harlequin," Stephanie said. "Great choice. There are some compelling arguments where they originate from among breeders and historians. Some say the Netherlands because of its Dutch roots, some say France where it was exhibited in 1887, and some say they come from my homeland Japan. I don't really care, I'm just happy these silly rabbits exist."

"Wow," Elyse said. "I don't even know where to start."

"You're my kind of people," Stephanie said. "Did you know American soldiers ate Harlequins during World War II? Cutting them into neat slices, dipping them in a variety of sauces. Rather gruesome and unethical if you ask me."

"I had no idea," Victoria chimed in.

"Me either," Karmina said.

"So hold on, you're Japanese?" Victoria asked. "I thought you were Korean."

"Stop being racist," Karmina said, glaring at her friend. Sometimes she couldn't believe the words that spilled out of Victoria's mouth. It was as if she had no home training, no self-awareness about the way her words came across.

"I'm not," Victoria said, she walked over and tossed her phone in the basket. "I swear."

"What about you?" Stephanie walked up to Karmina with a stupid grin plastered on her face, stretching the basket forward. "You look like a tough cookie."

"Sure," Karmina tossed her phone in the basket.

"Tough cookies come from tough childhoods," Stephanie said. "Don't forget that dough can be kneaded into new shapes and new forms. You don't have to let yourself harden over the sweet parts that I can see under the surface."

Karmina's jaw dropped and she was at a loss for words. She did have a tough childhood, watching her brothers, making sure they wouldn't get into trouble while her parents were at work all the time. She served as the third parent in the house, responsibility slammed on her little shoulders, her inner child crumpled up into a ball somewhere in her gut. Triggered, she yearned for another shot to wash away the untethered feeling vibrating through her body.

"Hold on, girls. Let me put this basket away somewhere safe and sound, and then the true fun will begin."

6

Maximoto's Escape

SOMETHING SHADOWY SQUIRMED INSIDE the crook of Stephanie's arm and Elyse struggled to figure out what type of animal it was. Knowing how eccentric the girl was, it could be anything. Maybe a weasel, a raccoon, an otter, a marten, or quite possibly a mink. Stephanie stepped into the light and the dimming sun rays revealed a fat bunny.

"Aww that bunny is the sweetest thing in the world," Elyse bent in close, gushing over the jackrabbit, scratching its head.

"Say thank you, Maximoto," Stephanie took the jackrabbit's small paw and waved it at the group of girls and spoke in a fake baby voice. "Thank you."

"I wished I had my phone," Victoria whined. "I would have taken some cute photos for the gram. I'm sure I would have got a ton of likes too."

Stephanie Kusuma caressed the bunny's plump belly. "Did you know black-tailed jackrabbits are famous for their large ears? Not only are they cute, but functional. Their ears have blood vessels that can widen, which allows greater control of their body temperature, keeping them cool on a hot day. Isn't that fascinating?"

"Totally," Elyse said, enjoying the bunny talk. "You're like a bunny encyclopedia. Where did you learn all of this knowledge?"

"Thank you," Stephanie said, petting the jackrabbit's soft coat. "I'm obsessed with bunnies. Got one when I was three and the rest was history. I study books, watch documentaries, and visit caretakers, soaking up as much knowledge as I can."

"That's amazing!" Elyse said gushing. She had to admit this girl was kind of strange, but she tried her best not to judge people, especially on the first meeting. Maybe she was neurodivergent, but that was no reason to minimize her good qualities. Something about Stephanie was alluring and she was so sincere and pretty.

The jackrabbit hopped out of Stephanie's hands and disappeared into the tall grass, flashes of its white coat could be seen bounding towards the bales of hay.

"Maximoto got impatient," Stephanie sighed. "He's throwing a hissy fit with his big self. Happens from time to time."

"What do you mean?" Karmina asked.

"He's going into the labyrinth for a good frolic," Stephanie said. "However, it's time for us to play a game. A good ole fashioned Easter egg hunt."

"I thought that was for kids?" Victoria said. "And it's getting dark out. How do you expect us to find these eggs?"

"Glad you asked," Stephanie said. "Rest assured the eggs will find you with a little help from some light."

Stephanie dug into the sharp V of her cleavage and pulled out a small black device and pressed a red button. Fairy lights wrapped around the haystacks glowed and pulsated like the veins of some Lovecraftian beast, moving to a stygian rhythm. They illuminated the otherwise square shapes and the entrances of the labyrinth.

"You're two steps ahead," Karmina said.

"I know," Stephanie said. "That's what my grandma used to say. She's a pop artist. Pretty talented if you ask me."

"Cool," Elyse said, wondering what percentage of words Stephanie spoke were fabrications, delusions, or pieces of truth. "What do these Easter eggs look like?"

Stephanie unscrewed the cap on her bottle wedged between her armpit and tossed back a hefty swig. She wiped her mouth with the back of her hand, a concoction of herbs and alcohol smearing across her fingers.

"Wormwood," Karmina said, excitedly. "You're drinking wormwood."

"Isn't that illegal?" Victoria asked.

"Why would it be illegal?" Elyse asked. "This is the first time I've heard of this."

Elyse wasn't a big drinker. A lot of times she drank in social settings to get rid of her anxiety and sometimes just to fit in with the crowd. She hated feeling out of place and loved keeping the peace. Wormwood sounded Southern and gothic, and she didn't understand what the big deal was.

"Wormwood contains hallucinogenic properties, specifically thujone" Stephanie explained. "Scientists claim this is a myth and they might be right. However, my Obaasan taught me a family recipe handed down from generation to generation. Unique herbs like mugwort, San Pedro cactus slices, and a venomous snake carcass will enhance the liquor and crack open the veil."

"That can't be safe," Karmina said, looking concerned. "Cracking open veils…"

Karmina's concern was infectious, and Elyse felt worried about their host for the first time. Until this moment, Elyse dismissed her friends, so badly wanting to indulge her desire to connect back with her childhood joy associated with Easter. Maybe she should have listened to their worries. Guilt wrapped around her throat, pushing down on her chest. She wanted to apologize, but she felt like they were too deep in this situation to reverse course. This was turning out to be one hell of a night.

"I've done this yearly, and I haven't had any issues," Stephanie said, draining the rest of the bottle. She tossed it into the grass. "My mental faculties are balanced, and my emotions are like the ocean, swift and rising."

Karmina shot Elyse a look, the kind of look only close friends could interpret like an ancient language. Elyse shrugged, playing dumb. Karmina scoffed in return and Victoria looked completely disinterested in their back and forth.

"Let's get this damn thing started before this liquor starts wearing off," Victoria said.

"That's the spirit!" Stephanie clapped her hands following behind Victoria. Karmina did a light jog to catch up, falling into a steady pace alongside Victoria.

Looks like it's really happening. One step closer to the Frolicking, whatever that means.

A strange sense of exhilaration took hold of Elyse as they walked towards the haystacks. She felt like she was stepping into the unknown and throwing caution to the wind. The tequila sloshed around her stomach, and she picked up the pace and looked up at the moon shining overhead. She wondered if her boyfriend was doing okay.

Three entrances opened up to the girls and Elyse had no idea which one she should take. Was this some type of test or was this just an elaborate Easter egg hunt like Stephanie said?

"You said this is a labyrinth," Elyse said. "What's the purpose of this? I never heard of labyrinths in Easter traditions."

"Good question," Stephanie said. "In Medieval times, people thought the labyrinth was a path to God, but it has always served as a divine tool for mankind. A tool for spiritual growth and enlightenment. Jung might say we're entering the womb and will come out reborn and renewed."

"Well which one is it?" Karmina asked.

"Was Jung right?" Elyse asked.

"We're about to find out," Stephanie said. "Choose whichever path calls out to you. There are no wrong answers here. Each one of you showed up for reasons beyond this 3D realm. You answered the universe's call."

Elyse stepped into the middle path and didn't see either of the girls follow. She assumed Victoria chose the left while Karmina chose the right path, visualizing her friends bickering amongst themselves beforehand. Imagining the girls walking into the circular haystacks seemed unsettling, Elyse kept expecting one of her friends to pop out, but she was alone.

She walked through the path, following the curves and pulled out a wisp of hay, twisting the yellow straws into new shapes, enjoying the tactile feeling. It's better than doing nothing and letting her thoughts get the best of her. Like what if she got lost? What if this was some type of elaborate trap? She couldn't even play music off her phone or make a call if she broke her ankle in a rabbit hole. God knows that would be a terrible stroke of luck.

Something shifted in her tote bag and she looked inside, remembering the bear spray her boyfriend forced her to bring. Maybe he had some intuitive foresight because this brought her a sense of immense calm, knowing she was equipped with a weapon. She didn't think she'd have to use it, but it was good to have nonetheless.

Something weighty scratched her left shoe and she nearly jumped out of her skin. Heart hammering in her chest, Stephanie wrapped her hand around the can and noticed Maximoto chewing on hay, staring up at her with black eyes. Wet and gleaming.

"Maximoto, you scared the living daylights out of me," Elyse bent down and petted his hide. "You almost got blasted with bear mace. I would have blinded you for life and I'm sure your mother Stephanie wouldn't be too pleased with that, now would she?"

The jackrabbit took off, sprinting into the shadows, obviously not wanting to be caught.

"Always in such a rush," Elyse said, standing back up. She missed her own bunny Yon Yon and wondered how he was doing home alone. She knew he had plenty of food, water, and treats, but she still worried about him as if he were her son. Brandi was looking after him and that relieved the tension in her neck, knowing her roommate would take good care of him like she had done so many times in the past.

Elyse continued walking and noticed something sticking out of a hay bale. She moved closer and confirmed her suspicions. Excitement fluttered in her stomach, and she found a brightly colored egg. Jumping up and down, she felt like she won a gameshow and had become wildly triumphant. The egg fell from her hands and cracked. Orange goo oozed outside the shell, messing up the food dye and decorative patterns.

"Damn, I need to be more careful."

She thought about cracking it all the way open, curiosity nagging at her in the worst way possible. She wasn't sure if she should wait to catch up with her friends or if she was allowed to see the treasure inside, assuming there was a treasure to begin with.

Fuck it, it's my prize. Might as well enjoy it.

Elyse dug her fingers into the crack, ripping away pieces of the eggshell. She felt giddy as a kid on Christmas morning, savagely ripping away wrapping paper, trying to get to the good stuff. An object wrapped in gold aluminum paper shone in the moonlight. She dropped the rest of the egg and inspected the mysterious object, moving it underneath the pulsing lights around her.

She unwrapped the object and discovered a chocolate egg inside. Milk chocolate she assumed purely by the coloring. Pinching it between her index and thumb, she plopped it in her mouth. Her face scrunched up as she chewed the bitter-flavored chocolate and swallowed it down. She wondered what else was in the ingredients besides the actual chocolate since she could taste herbs in the mix. Part of her was concerned that she had been drugged by Stephanie and she felt a weird combination of anger and frustration.

Taking a deep breath, she calmed herself down, trying not to think the worst of their host. Maybe it was a Japanese chocolate with a unique flavoring inside. No reason to freak out especially when she didn't have the answers. Her stomach gurgled and the tequila coursed through her veins, as she continued moving deeper into the labyrinth.

7

The Left Hand Path

SOMEWHERE IN THE DISTANCE, an owl hooted, and Victoria wondered if she made a mistake by picking the left-hand path and not following the others. She read somewhere that the left was associated with satanic rituals and dark magic, witchcraft done in the dead of night. Was she manifesting something ill-advised in this maze? Something that would creep out of the darkness? She pushed the dark thoughts into the recesses of her mind and found herself running her fingertips along the black wires wrapped around the hay bales. They reminded her of charred veins, the only source of light in the shadowy labyrinth.

Dim memories of Christmas time crept through her mind as the lights flashed green and then changed to a crimson red. Most Christmases had been a series of nightmares for her in the past, her parents buying her toys she didn't want and exercise equipment every year until she lost weight. One year there was the weighted purple jump rope she could barely lift, the next was a pair of running shoes, the next a yoga mat and small weights. It made her feel like a burden rather than a child, a fat feminine sack of lard walking through life and trying her best not to be seen, but wishing desperately for acknowledgment from the two figures who brought her into the world.

She wiped a tear under her eye, barely registering the emotional wounds reopening inside her chest, foolishly assuming they had healed after she'd left home for college and had become an adult or so she thought.

"What am I doing here?" Victoria said, kicking an empty plastic pop bottle.

"You're exactly where the universe wants you to be. Searching for answers and playing games," Stephanie said, seemingly appearing out of nowhere. "Kismet."

"Not you," Victoria said, wiping her face and hoping the girl didn't see her crying.

"Not me, not I, just a girl frolicking through the night, guiding you towards a fertile beginning," Stephanie said in a sing-song voice, something plucked straight out of a lost Disney film helmed by David Cronenberg.

"Why do you talk like that?" Victoria asked, tired of the shenanigans. She resisted the urge to be mean, swallowing down the beast that fought to surface. Her mask was slipping, but she didn't know if she cared for this girl to know the real her or the façade she showed to her friends.

"I'm being authentic, you should try it out some time. It's refreshing, it's liberating and the only way I know how to be. That's part of the reason I live out here. I'm not corrupted by social media or society's sick programming."

"Fair enough," Victoria said, knowing this weird girl saw right through her. She felt like a sheet of glass, transparent and hollow. It made her woozy and she wished she could grab some liquor to drown the emotions percolating inside her gut.

"We all wear masks, you know," Stephanie said, spinning in circles, the hem of her dress slicing through the night air. "I just chose to throw mine away, burning them in the forgotten flame. Watching the ashes get swallowed up by the earth."

A flower flew out of Stephanie's hair, uncoiling from the waterfall braid, viciously snatched away by the wind. Something about her movements was erratic yet graceful. Victoria wondered if she had been a ballerina when she was little, practicing movements over and over, perfecting the timing and repetition like a spin-up doll. Toes aching inside shoes too small and restrictive for her delicate feet.

"The forgotten flame…" Victoria repeated the words and felt goosebumps raise along her forearm. *What the hell does that mean?*

"Yeah, burn baby burn," Stephanie said, eye twitching. "I'm no arsonist, but boy do we know about the flame."

Victoria nodded and followed the girl deeper into the labyrinth, figuring she had to know the lay of the land since she lived here. A reasonable assumption.

"These eggs, where are these eggs you were talking about earlier?" Victoria asked. "Did you hide them yourself?"

"No, silly," Stephanie chuckled. "The rabbits orchestrated this. They hide the eggs every year. They always do and always will. It's custom."

This bitch must be off her rocker or poppin pills. I heard there was an opioid epidemic in the Midwest, but I've never met one these addicts.

Victoria could give two fucks if this girl was neurodivergent or not. She was cuckoo, far too many screws missing in her head and Victoria was forced to put her trust in her.

Note to self, do not come back to Plainfield, Illinois, even in the daylight. Villages are not for me. I don't care if there's a cute boy hiding out here. No coming back.

Victoria followed along and found a hole in the hay bale. Darkness coated the opening, and she couldn't help but feel a pull towards it. She reached her hand inside and pulled out an egg that was slick with a foreign substance. It had stripes and weird symbols drawn on the outside. Reminded her of something you would see in a witchcraft documentary. Sigil was the word she was looking for.

"You found one," Stephanie clapped her hands and hugged Victoria tightly. "I wasn't sure if you would find one with your bad attitude to be honest, but you did it. Oh boy, did you pull off the impossible. Congratulations."

Something about the hug triggered a memory inside Victoria's psyche, rising to the surface like discarded trash from her preteen years. A time when all she yearned for was affection, affection from her parents. A simple hug. Isn't that what most children want? To be embraced, to be seen, to be acknowledged and to be loved. She walked up to her mom before leaving out the front door for the school bus, arms outstretched. Her mother recoiled, stepping back, scrunching her rotund face into a punctuation mark she couldn't decipher, but one she could feel.

Disgust and disdain painted across her wrinkled features.

"Get away from me," her mom barked. "Not until you lose five more pounds. Only then will you deserve a hug."

Victoria threw her hood over her head and fled the house, wanting to reject this new prize. Affection serving as a treat for giving into her mother's demands.

"What do I do now?" Victoria said, fighting to suppress the old emotions. She couldn't look Stephanie in the eye. The intimacy would make her explode.

"Crack it open and enjoy your winnings," Stephanie said. "You deserve it."

Even though Victoria felt slightly patronized, she did feel a sense of accomplishment swelling inside of her and she enjoyed the enthusiasm dripping off Stephanie. The sentiment was sincere and honest and she rarely received that from the people closest to her. She wiped a tear away and pulled out her keys and jabbed one in the egg, cracking the shell. Then she ripped it apart with her fingertips, digging until a bronze-wrapped object was revealed.

"Ohhhhhhhh la la, you fancy, miss Victoria. Open it up."

Victoria smiled and gingerly unwrapped the bronze foil, discovering a small chocolate egg. The texture was dark, so she assumed it was dark chocolate, which was something she secretly loved. She pushed it into her mouth and wrapped her tongue around the outside enjoying the taste.

"The moon is massive," Stephanie said, gesturing towards the darkening sky. "Look at her shining in all her lunar brilliance. Can you taste her light?"

"I don't know…" Victoria said, confused. The egg traveled down her esophagus and made its way into her stomach. Her body felt funny, ticklish and vibrant. Every hair stood on end. "I feel weird."

"That means the egg is working," Stephanie said. "Fabolous.

"The egg is working…" Victoria said, paranoia clutching her heart. She rubbed her arms, feeling a slight chill in the air. "What does that mean? Did you drug me?"

"I would never do that, but I wouldn't put it past the rabbits. They're a nefarious sort, but don't be too hard on them. They mean well."

"How can drugging someone mean well?" Victoria asked, eyes feeling wetter than usual or was she on the verge of tears? She couldn't tell.

"They're doing what they're designed to do. Opening the doors of perception that are usually closed to most," Stephanie said, sniffing the air. "You and your friends are fortunate to be here. The time is approaching…"

"Like shrooms, like Aldous Huxley? I can't," Victoria said, panic beginning to sink in. "I've never done hallucinogens. I need to throw up, like yesterday."

Victoria bent over, sticking a long index finger down her throat, a pink fingernail clawing at her tonsils, remembering the routine in her teenage years, afraid the fat might come back at any time to consume her. She hated the smell, the acidic burn in her throat, the mucus dripping down her lips, the vomit floating in the toilet bowl.

Bulimia. She hated that fucking word just as much as she hated the word moist. It made her cringe, made her feel like there was something wrong with her. She wished it was something cute, something she could embrace and wrap around herself like an emotional support dog instead of a label that made people look at you with unease and trepidation.

At this moment, she could care less if the crazy pretty girl watched her in her most vulnerable state. She had no attachment to the girl, no friendship, no bond. There was nothing to prove. She wasn't big on drugs and had only tried coke three times since being in college. Other than that, she was clean and enjoyed being in control of her body. The thought of hallucinating in this big ass cornfield made her want to leap out of her skin.

"It's too late," Stephanie said, clamping a hand on Victoria's shoulder and giving it a firm squeeze. "It's entered your bloodstream and many of these decisions were made long before you stepped foot on this cornfield. Why waste your energy, silly?"

Victoria ignored her, retching and gagging as she struggled to throw up the contents inside her stomach. She only managed to spit out clumps of phlegm and the entire ordeal made her hyper-aware of the tequila still coursing through her body.

This isn't working. Why the fuck isn't anything coming up? Why did you let Elyse talk you into being here in the first place? Stupid!

She wiped a layer of sweat off her forehead and felt the wetness soaking her armpits. Thankfully, her surroundings looked the same and nothing seemed to be on the outskirts of reality quite yet and no cute men could see her at her worst.

"Are you done yet?" Stephanie asked, arms crossed and feet apart in a wide stance. "We have places to go."

"Yeah, I think so."

"Good, let's go find the girls on the other side. I hope they found their eggs as well. Isn't this so much fun?"

"I guess," Victoria said with a sinking feeling of dread slowly being lowered into her stomach like a cheap wooden casket, ready to crack at any moment. She steeled herself for the chaotic break, the oncoming cuts, the inevitable splinters, and the bloody hallucinations that she prayed would continue to be figments of her imagination and not something much more troubling.

Her stomach churned and a snake of anxiety slithered through her throat as she became aware of the dryness of her mouth, and the sheer weight of her tongue, thirsting for water.

8

Rabbit Holes

KARMINA ADJUSTED HER HAIR and almost forgot the entrance she took. She didn't worry about it too much since she usually had her wits about her in any situation. Stephanie had called this a labyrinth, but she figured the girl may have been severely mistaken. Who would go out of their way to construct a labyrinth in the middle of nowhere? It didn't make any sense.

What the girl meant to say was maze. Had to be an oversight. Karmina knew the words were significantly different but shared a mystery-like quality. That had to be it. A simple mistake.

Cornfields and fairs always had cute mazes. How hard could this one be?

She moved through the maze, walking with purpose, taking long strides. Walking as if she knew the lay of the land. Corner after corner. Bend after bend. The lights pulsated like the stretched ventricles and valves of a heart. Strands of hay gleamed in the light and reminded Karmina of small knives. Sharp and jabbing. Something about the night seemed alive, but she attributed that to the alcohol. Nothing else made sense.

Part of her felt like she was being extra and that the weird girl Stephanie was getting to her. Not much scared Karmina outside of spiders, extreme bouts of pain, and death. She had experienced so much of these qualities in her short time on earth—darkness and cornfields were the least of her worries.

That's when she spotted it—the egg. It lay inside an abandoned bird's nest on a haystack. Wild grass, twigs, leaves, and hay were tightly coiled together in a dark brown spiral. Karmina wondered if the birds were still alive or if they migrated down South. She figured Elyse would know and filed these questions away in the back of her head to ask later. Her hand wrapped around a blue egg with white specks on the outside. She couldn't tell if this design was on purpose or by accident. Stephanie's voice rang in her head, giving her a pleasant reminder.

My grandma's a pop artist.

Maybe Stephanie had artistic talents too. What was she doing living in the middle of nowhere, letting her talents go to waste? She seemed eccentric and pretty. Two qualities that should make her a standout and a surefire success in the art world. Karmina pictured her hosting a gallery showing, entitled men in business suits and women in intoxicating dresses drinking vintage wine, and offering up large sums of money for her paintings.

That's what should have been happening instead of telling girls to wander through a maze. These hypothetical situations made her smile, the fantasy distracting her from the fact that she had found an egg. She sensed that she was getting closer to the finish line, feeling this fact inside her gut.

Karmina saw a trio of holes, in front of her. She assumed only one thing dug them—rabbits.

Rabbit holes. Dark gaping openings in the softly packed earth two feet in front of her. She remembered Stephanie mentioning digging some. Were these her handiwork? And why did she help them when she said the rabbits weren't to be trusted? Her head throbbed the longer she searched for the elusive answer, so she massaged her forehead with her thumbs. Something instinctual told her to steer clear of the holes and she continued moving forward.

She swore she saw something pale dip beneath the earth as she glanced back, feeling uneasy about the holes despite the growing distance between her and the openings. The ground beneath her feet seemed to rumble and she picked up the pace, moving into a sprint, unsure as to what pursued her beneath the surface.

Karmina sprinted across the uneven terrain, taking a sharp turn, and running clear from the maze. She stood on a large flat rock and inspected the ground for any disturbances. Placing her hands behind her head, opening her lungs, Karmina sucked in mouthfuls of night air until her breathing calmed down.

She struggled to imagine what subterranean creature lay beneath the earth. Logic told her it was a rabbit since they dug the holes, but something seemed off. Anything could crawl into those spaces and who was to say they were native to this land? Maybe it was an invasive species that had infiltrated the soil or perhaps it was a mammal that had been here long before the village was erected. Something that reigned over this space in the daylight, but was driven beneath the surface for nefarious purposes.

The train of thought made Karmina's head swim and her stomach queasy. She continued scanning the earth, wondering if she saw something that normal eyes couldn't due to whatever substance was flowing through her system. Insects trilled and the night felt alive with something that made Karmina's skin crawl. She hoped the other girls would be joining her before the last solid fragments of her mind disintegrated.

9

Last Exit on the Right

ELYSE TOOK A LEFT and then a right or was it a
diagonal shortcut? She couldn't quite tell anymore.
Her sense of direction had gone wonky since she'd eaten
that egg and she didn't remember the labyrinth seeming
so large and sprawling from the outside looking in.

The varicose vein lights pulsated a soft blue, seemingly
brighter than before and more embedded in the walls of
the labyrinth. She struggled to distinguish the wires, the
black cords that must be hanging outside of the hay bales,
but she couldn't even when she got close. They blended
inside the dried grass, looking like the internal chambers
of an unknown beast instead of a fun maze.

The walls seemed to tighten at times and at other
junctures, it contracted and expanded. She never
experienced anything like it. There were points she felt

as if she was inside the lining of the labyrinth's stomach, being digested in strange ways, being pushed deeper into its system.

She walked around a grey rock that seemed familiar, and a plastic Walgreens bag billowed in the wind, barely holding onto a sharp piece of hay jabbing through a handle. This made Elyse remember all the times her parents took her to Walgreens as a child. The shelves seemed so large and full of wonder. She begged them for stuffed rabbits, bunny-shaped chocolates, colorful plastic eggs, fake hay, and more. They indulged her wishes several times, and the holiday ballooned in her heart.

This was only part of her holiday joy, but this was something she missed, pulling on her heartstrings. Family was so important to her and being with the girls helped, but it wasn't the same. She wiped a tear as she reached what seemed like the end of the labyrinth.

The exit stretched wider than the rest of the spaces she navigated and she felt like she could breathe easier. Moving down a hill, Elyse spotted three dark figures. She wondered if this was Stephanie, Victoria, and Karmina. It had to be, but part of her was scared that this trio could have been someone else, someone waiting to murder her.

Pushing the paranoid thoughts aside, Elyse calmly moved closer and her hunch proved to be right. Karmina, Victoria, and Stephanie seemed to be talking amongst themselves and tension was thick in the air.

"She fucking drugged us, Karmina!" Victoria shouted pointing her finger at Stephanie who seemed unphased by the accusations.

"Is this true?" Karmina asked.

Elyse watched silently as all eyes seemed to be thrust upon Stephanie.

"I did nothing of the sort. Ask the rabbits. The rabbits know the truth, the rabbits hid the eggs."

"But what's inside?" Victoria asked, hands on her hips. "I feel like I'm seeing shit."

Stephanie looked around like she was about to let the girls in on a massive secret. She spoke in a hushed tone, "Natural ingredients, catalysts to break down doors in your perception. Only the rabbits have access to these plants. Don't ask, don't tell."

"Fuck does that mean?" Victoria whined.

"You know what that means," Karmina scoffed. "We're trippin off some potent drugs. Might as well enjoy it."

"Excuse me, girls, while I grab something essential for the next phase," Stephanie said, before skipping away. "I hope you like music."

Karmina and Victoria bickered, barely paying attention to Elyse's existence. Her heart hurt as she felt almost non-existent, and the holiday joy was seeping out of her veins.

Elyse couldn't move her mouth and something about the darkness stretching into the grassy field seemed relentless and yawning.

10

Divine Heirlooms

S TEPHANIE RETURNED FROM THE outhouse with something wrapped in a red Kakefuton blanket. It was the size of a baby and the girls seemed to be readying themselves for the unveiling.

"It's time, girls," Stephanie bent down and unraveled the object, revealing an oversized shell. "This is an Australian trumpet shell, which used to house one of the largest gastropods in the world. The shell was soaked in dragon's blood, nanazuna, and nipplewort for seven days and seven nights by my mother, my mother's mother, and her mother before her."

"A heirloom," Karmina said, enraptured by the moment. Her voice felt ten times bigger inside her body, reverberating through her chest.

"Exactly that. This is a precious heirloom, a divine musical instrument, a tool used to tear down the programming that leaves us blind, and rip open the veil so we can frolic freely with little to no interference."

"Interference?" Elyse asked.

"Complicated and boring information. Just know there are blockades in our dimension, quantum foam, and magical impasses. What we've done tonight has readied ourselves for the next step. I just have to play a song. Are you girls ready to frolic?"

"Yes, but we don't even know what this frolicking is?" Elyse said, excitement rising through her chest.

"Frolicking is your birthright as women. I mean you're still girls, but after tonight you will be reborn and spit out as women. *Adult* women," Stephanie said, her left eye twitching. "You'll be surer of yourselves, more confident, and you'll step into your true power. The fear and doubt will fall away like old skins."

"Reborn…" Victoria said, playing around with the idea.

"I still don't quite understand this," Karmina said, fear wrapping around her throat. "I don't know if I want to do this…"

Stephanie's eye twitched even harder and her head cocked to the side. "Have you ever been obliterated by nature, your sense of self consumed by an open field? It's an enlightening experience, one that can bring about rebirth, wholeness, true womanhood. I can see the innocence in your eyes, the fear of tomorrow, the hesitancy in the way you slouch, the lack of intimacy with your bodies, your own power..."

"Hold up, what are the rules? I feel like there are rules."

"Silly me, I almost forgot about the rules," Stephanie hit her forehead with palm. "Rule number one--Do not cut corners. Rule number two--do not lie. Rule number three--Honesty is the best policy. Rule number four--Do not overstay your welcome. Rule number five--When in doubt, frolic. And last, but not least, remember this is all happening for you, not to you."

"What happens if we break the rules or we forget to follow one?" Victoria asked. "There's usually consequences."

"Bad things, girls. Very bad things, but don't worry, you're college students," Stephanie said, caressing the shell. "You're educated. You have big brains so you should be fine."

The girls looked at one another, unsaid messages passing between them. The type of communication only long-time friends possess.

"Elyse, what do you think?" Karmina said. "It's your call. I trust you."

"We're doing it," Elyse said, nodding with a grim determination. "Let's frolic."

Stephanie nodded and raised the shell upward, the pointed portion sliding in between her moist lips. She inhaled and she blew. Cheeks growing round and full of air. She blew into the trumpet and a beautiful, yet somber tune spilled out, vibrating through the field, overpowering the sounds of nature around them. She played for about ten minutes straight, but it only felt like three.

They all stood there, waiting for something to happen, too afraid to fuck something up with their words. Stephanie tossed the shell aside and began skipping and looked behind her, waiting for the girls to follow.

Elyse was the first to skip, fearlessly bounding into the air, enraptured by the Easter spirit, followed by Karmina, and lastly, Victoria taking the rear. It felt funny at first to Victoria, who worried that she drank too much liquor and that she might vomit, but she was surprised to find that her stomach was fine. And most surprisingly, she was having fun, not forced fake fun she put on, but genuine joy rippled through her frame.

They clutched hands and the time spent in the sky with each hop seemed to stretch further and further. An immense amount of joy took hold of Victoria, and she felt light as a feather. The girls giggled and laughed, twirling through the field.

Black dots bounced in the distance and Victoria thought she was overheating, and the darkness was playing with her vision. Perhaps she needed some water to sober up or maybe her mind was playing tricks on her, but she didn't think her vision would start deteriorating so soon at her young age. Both her parents wore glasses and couldn't see a damn thing without them. Still, Victoria began to doubt it was an orbital issue since the black dots grew in size. Looking as if they could hold 30 people inside comfortably.

Stephanie continued frolicking around the field without a care in the world. And she skipped right into the center of one dot and disappeared.

This stopped Victoria in her tracks, but Karmina and Elyse continued holding hands. Their eyes were closed and they both were stuck in their own worlds. Should she say something? Did it even matter? Even the fear she knew she *should* feel right now was missing, and not too soon after, the compulsion to frolic came back to her. Her legs bent down as if they had their own mind, knees bent, and she vaulted back into the air. The joy returned and Victoria figured the black dots must be hallucinations. They couldn't hurt her. Why else would Stephanie jump inside one?

Victoria jumped over and over and over, bounding into the sky. She didn't find her breathing to be heavy or labored. Instead, it felt like she had an endless amount of cardio, endurance, and stamina. A set of iron lungs. The runner's high of runner's highs. She frolicked through the field, skipping headfirst into a black dot.

Passing through the dot, which was now a huge circle tinged lava red, felt like moving through a thin layer of jelly, a film that she easily broke through. She tumbled forward, nearly falling flat on her face. What saved her were two yellow pumpkins that her hands smashed through. Strangely enough, they smelled like sweet apple pie with a hint of cinnamon. Her hands came away covered in wet sticky seeds. She wiped it on the ground, which didn't feel like ordinary soil. Something about the consistency felt drier and the plant life around her seemed to be stiff in a sense, lacking life.

That's when she noticed a ton of pumpkins surrounding her, varying in size. Some were as big as a car while others were as a small as mouse. She assumed she stumbled upon a pumpkin patch, but she never experienced one quite like this. Running her hands along the grooves of a massive pumpkin, she wondered how these came to be.

They must be injected with something like GMOs or maybe this is an experiment.

The other strange quality about these pumpkins was the black dots decorating each pumpkin. She thought they were painted on, but as she dug into one with her long fingernail, she noticed this was a natural part of their composition. Flicking pieces of the pumpkin aside, she wished Karmina and Elyse were here. They might actually be able to make sense of this situation. Loneliness wrapped around her, and she realized she hadn't been alone in a long time especially being on campus.

Victoria shielded her eyes from the sunlight or what she thought was the sun, but she struggled to find the orb in the blue sky. Something about the sky looked smeared and artificial like a movie set. However, the light felt warm on her skin, much warmer than the chill she felt outside.

She moved deeper into the pumpkin patch and turned around, looking for the entrance, but it was no longer there. Panic took hold of her, and she began hyperventilating, picturing herself trapped in this space for the rest of eternity. She wished she stuck to her guns earlier and kept her phone, but she gave in to the peer pressure from the other girls. Falling to her knees, she ugly cried, sniffling, but a hunger rumbled in her stomach.

The pumpkins seemed to be calling out to her, despite her not being the biggest fan of pumpkins. She enjoyed a pumpkin spice latte on occasion and pumpkin pie, but she never went out of her way to seek it out. Still,

Victoria took out her lip gloss, searching for a sense of familiarity, and slowly applied it. She smacked her lips together, hoping the application was on point since there were no mirrors anywhere.

I hope I don't look like a clown.

The lip gloss slipped out of her hands and rolled next to a bush. A cute rabbit popped out and sniffed it before snatching it up with its small mouth. It took off.

"Hold on!" Victoria yelled. "That's not a carrot. That's my lip gloss. Come back here!"

The rabbit paused, waiting for Victoria to catch up. At the very moment she bent down to grab her lip gloss, the rabbit took off again. This tiring cycle continued for another ten minutes until it pivoted left into a circle full of massive pumpkins, disappearing.

This motherfucker.

Victoria took a second to catch her breath and sprinted past the pumpkins, looking for the rabbit. She slipped and tumbled forward into a large, gaping black hole. As she fell deeper into the darkness, she caught a glimpse of the bunny perched over the edge, looking down at her with her lip gloss clasped between its teeth.

11

Oswaldo's Unlikely Call

A MURKY YELLOW DOT stretched wide in front of Karmina. It seemed to loom over her, engulfing her vision like a futuristic flat screen, maybe eight feet tall and six feet wide. A wet film seemed to ripple in front of her, dark bubbles sliding across the vertical surface, and she heard laughter and muffled chatter. Something about the muddied voices seemed familiar and another laugh made her heart ache. It was her brothers. All four of them waiting for her on the other side. She was sure of it.

Something about this impossible moment made her head woozy and she tried to make sense of it. Alcohol and bits of spoiled rye bread sloshed around her stomach as she took a step forward, feeling the portal's invitation to enter. She remembered books like *The Chronicles of Narnia*, the kids who stepped across the threshold and the witch on the other side offering sweet chocolates. Memories of her brothers growing older and moving across the country to get married, start new jobs, further their education, and carve out their own vibrant lives flooded her mind. She turned around, forcing herself to step away from the yellow dot, tears brimming in her eyes.

"Mina, where you going?" Her oldest brother Oswaldo, called out to her. She turned back, wiping a tear away, and struggled to make out his round face obscured by the sickly yellow veil. A nagging curiosity and loyalty to her bloodline, caused her to forget where she was and she went into the portal, throwing caution to the wind, stepping into the void headfirst.

The air was different, clearer in a sense. Like she could breathe deeper and take in more oxygen in her lungs. Felt good. She might as well have been in the mountains, at a higher altitude. Instead, she found herself inside a spacious living room with a large couch, a sofa, and a couple of reading chairs. A clear cookie jar with a crack on the outside, the same crack from the cookie jar in her childhood home, sat on the coffee table and she popped it open. Fresh oatmeal cookies stacked on top one another, the smell made her stomach rumble. She wasn't sure if these were safe to eat, but they seemed fine enough. Sticking her hand into the jar and pulling one out, Karmina yelped as she watched it crumble in her hand, making a mess on the floor. Thinking nothing of it, she grabbed another and the second cookie crumbled as well. She did it one more time, thinking the third time would be the charm, but the baked good disintegrated into a powdery mess.

Karmina sighed heavily, feeling tricked out of a sweet snack, and tried to brush it off.

Maybe it wasn't meant to be.

Karmina continued exploring the space, gym shoes sinking into the carpet with each step, wet and pliable, giving her the sense of a domestic swamp frothing beneath her feet. She expected to smell mildew but found the unmistakable aroma of *tostones, carne mechada*, and *pisca andina* drifting from everywhere and nowhere at once.

This familiar smell made her mouth salivate and her stomach grumble as she continued walking across the carpet. She wondered where her siblings were and she missed her family's presence, the sense of togetherness they once shared. They must be hiding behind the strange furniture that seemed to be sprouting pale, bulbous shapes that resembled deformed yams. Small red dots stippled the outside of every object like a nasty infection.

Her legs grew tired, sloshing through the synthetic fibers that seemed to caress her feet and ankles.

"Oswaldo, stop playing around," Karmina called out, trying to lure her brothers out from their hiding places. "I heard you outside. No more games. I'm home."

Still no response and the word *outside* startled her. She couldn't see the entrance to this strange place any longer. Now that she thought about it, she couldn't feel the breeze or see the fields of grass or the cornfields or the girls or the weird Asian girl Stephanie who led them here. Karmina felt like she was fucked from all angles. Panic began setting in, but it dissolved as soon as she heard a familiar voice—one of her brothers.

"Calm down, Karmina. You're with family."

"Where are you?" she asked, feeling like was playing some demented form of Marco Polo with her siblings.

There was a canoe in the corner of the room that she hadn't seen before, constructed from the same yam material the couch shared. Two bulbous oars rested inside the boat. Small red dots speckled across the white wood that made her fearful of touching them, reminding her of poisonous spores. Despite this trepidation, something about this vessel called out to Karmina and she carefully stepped inside. She'd been inside dingy boats in her younger years, exploring small rivers in her homeland, enjoying the serene nature of the waters she navigated.

The yam-like walls constructing the corner of the living room split apart, snapping like twigs. The space opened up like a dream, revealing a watery substance that still blended in with the domestic environment. Lamps, books, picture frames, and knick-knacks floated in the substance.

Karmina stopped questioning the craziness around her, grabbed the oars, which seemed alive, and dipped them into the water, rotating them forward and rowing them back. She knew her brothers were out there and she was determined to be reunited with her siblings.

12

Mirrors Follow Me

DESPITE THE DRUGS RUNNING through her system and the joy flowing through her body, Elyse knew what *it* was the moment she stood in front of it. The large crackling circle that was once a dot in the distance was a portal. She could understand someone mistaking the entrance for a hallucination, a void, or a figment of the imagination, but it was deeper than that.

Sometimes you recognize things for what they are instinctively.

The portal hovered at the center of her chest and she could feel *it* calling out to her. It wasn't a whisper, an intrusive thought or a weird voice. Instead, it was a feeling, a compulsion to step inside. A soft invitation into the unknown, something that was attempting to pierce the thick skin of logic and reason.

Through half-slitted eyes and a cloud of bliss, she saw Stephanie disappear into the mouth of a yawning portal with no hesitation whatsoever. She figured Stephanie had done this countless times and had come out changed for the better. Elyse had no idea what was on the other side though. Was it an Easter paradise? Bunnies hopping through endless greenery, Easter egg hunts, or something more? Did this lead to a desert or would this lead her to an abandoned mall or something much worse?

Elyse carefully extended her index finger forward, wanting to test the waters of the darkness, and poked the rim of the dark portal, expecting to feel a sudden jerk or witness a ripple across the surface. She experienced none of these things. Her finger felt fine, and the weather didn't feel any different inside the space. Feeling bold, she folded her fingers into a fist and pushed it inside, followed by half an arm, expecting anything and everything to happen at once. Her heart beat like a wild horse bucking and she licked her lips, feeling the passage of time slowing down. On the verge of panic and what she assumed to be the prelude to a heart attack, she whipped her limb back outside, clutching it to her chest.

Inspecting her arm and hand, everything seemed the exact same and there were no changes whatsoever. She clenched and unclenched her fist, feeling the blood flow through her limb. Somewhat surprised by the lack of disturbances in the portal, she exhaled and her heartbeat returned to normal.

Seems safe enough…

The portal widened, stretching to knee level now, and the invitation to enter grew tremendously in Elyse's mind. She backed up a few feet to get a running start and took off at a light jog, speeding up. At the last second, she closed her eyes and leaped into the portal, landing on her feet perfectly, crouched down. The contents of her bag clanged against one another, coming to rest against her side.

French jazz played in the large room and this music put Elyse at ease. Colorful dots floated in the air, mirroring variegated galaxies, and black chandeliers hung down from the ceiling that seemed to extend into the sky. Mirrored walls, mirrored floors, mirrored squares, and mirrored boxes filled the space. Elyse smiled in awe as she took it all in.

Elyse's steps echoed throughout the room as she explored the space, running her hand across a mirror. The oils in her fingertips left a smudge, evidence of her humanity in such an alien space.

She looked at herself in the mirror and liked what she saw and did a little spin. Something bright white flashed across the floor and a bunny popped its head up sniffing the air.

"Follow me, human."

Elyse stopped in her tracks and questioned if she was hearing things. Bunnies couldn't talk, it had to be the easter egg she consumed earlier. Part of her hoped that she passed out in the maze and this was a strange dream, but she knew that foolish thinking and she had to accept the risk she took jumping into the portal in the first place—even if that meant bunnies talking. The bunny looked at her a moment and hopped through a space in the wall big enough for her and the bunny to fit through. Not wanting to be left behind, Elyse chased after the bunny, awkwardly running after the white flash of fur.

"Hold on a sec, slow down," Elyse said.

She entered the new space which resembled the last one except the French music picked up the pace, saxophone and violins becoming more rhythmic. The lighting in the room pulsed with a purple light. She couldn't find the source of the lighting and the colorful dots took on an unearthly texture. The bunny ran underneath two mirrored boxes and disappeared. Elyse got down on her hands and knees, looking for it. When she stood back up, she gasped.

"How do you like the new look?"

Her boyfriend Skylar sat on two squares, leaning back with his hands clasped behind his head as if the blocks were the most comfortable thing in the world, lounging. He wore blue jeans with fake paint splatter, white Vans, and an oversized Denim Tears t-shirt. His hair seemed shorter though, resembling the length he sported when they first met.

"Babe, when'd you get here? I thought you were at home?" Elyse said, dumbfounded by his sudden appearance.

"Easy. I pulled up."

"I didn't see you come inside the portal though. This doesn't make any sense."

Skylar waved his big hand, dismissing her. "Everything doesn't have to make sense. Aren't you happy I'm here?"

Elyse looked at her boyfriend who seemed to be normal, but something was off. Her intuition screamed at her to be careful, to keep him at an arm's distance. Knowing better, she ignored it, having to test the waters. She carefully approached him, and tugged on his cheek, squeezing the flesh, fully expecting it to rip away like a mask, but he grunted in pain, swatting her hand away.

"Lovebug, stop! That shit hurts. Don't treat me like my Polish grandma."

"Sorry, babe. Just had to test something."

"Test something else. Sheesh."

"I have a couple of questions so be patient with me. Did you see the bunny in here and when did you get your haircut?"

"No, I didn't see any bunnies in here. And I got my hair cut earlier today. Went and saw Deano. Gave me the hot towel treatment with a touch of eucalyptus. Refreshing."

"Cool."

"So tell me what you think."

"Looks cool."

"I don't believe you. I can hear it in your inflection. The words don't even sound sincere. You know you can be honest with me, right?"

"Yeah, of course." Elyse's stomach churned and she realized she wasn't being honest. She thought the cut was cute when she first met him, but now she had grown accustomed to his hair being longer. Plus, she didn't want to hurt his feelings.

"How about now?"

Elyse had somehow looked away for a mere moment and when she turned back, she saw Skylar was naked in the same position as before. His clothes were nowhere to be found and he stroked his throbbing cock in his hand. Veins covered his member and she felt herself getting turned on, a hint of wetness growing between her legs.

"Babe, where are your clothes at?"

"Answer the question."

"Babe."

"Don't deflect, answer the question," he said, tone hardening.

"I mean you look good, but I don't think this is the time and place."

"See, there you go with the halfway honest answers. Might as well spit on me and say it's raining."

"Babe, you're being mean and aggressive," she said sniffling, fighting back the tears begging to come out of her ducts. "Can we slow down a second?""So this is all about you now? Might as well be the Elyse show," Skylar said as his grip on his cock tightened and his stroke became more intense, working the shaft. "I just ask for a little honesty and you can't even give me that."

The dam broke and tears came down, blurring Elyse's vision. She wiped them with the back of her hands, unsure how she even got here. Usually, she and her boyfriend had great conflict resolution, so this sudden change caught her off guard and rocked her emotionally.

"Mernem djanit," he said, curling the corner of his mouth into a grin.

I will die on your body? When did Skylar learn Armenian? This made no sense whatsoever. The only language her boyfriend spoke was weights and English. She knew the romantic expression was meant to convey great love for her, but it had the opposite effect—shaking her up even more.

"How about now?"

Skylar was in a bunny suit now, that covered him from head to toe. It seemed pretty realistic to the point that even his eyes were black and gleaming. His nose twitched, sniffing the air, and his cock still throbbed in his hand.

"How can you breathe in that suit?" she asked, voice cracking. She was concerned about him, despite the onslaught of tears and the overwhelming lack of emotional control.

"Just fine."

"Now, you're being cold."

"Oh I'm being mean, I'm being aggressive, I'm being cold. Why can't I fucking be, Elyse? Why can't I have emotions? And why can't you get off your high horse and just be honest with me, huh?"

"You're scaring me, Sky…why don't take off that fake head so you can look me in the eyes. I'm feeling unsafe and this isn't like you."

"Take off the head?" he laughed. "You gotta be kidding me."

"I'm not…fine, I'll take it off for you."

Elyse cautiously walked up to Skylar and pushed her hands underneath his neck, searching for the line disconnecting the head from the rest of the body.

Found it.

Elyse lifted the furry head, which sounded like a suction cup being pulled off a glass table. It weighed a lot more than it looked, Elyse realized as she struggled to lift it over his head, and it landed on the mirrored floor with a thud. Cracks splintered outward and Elyse looked at her haggard reflection fragmented into an abhorrent portrait underneath her feet.

Skylar grinned at her, white teeth gleaming in stark contrast to his red glistening muscles exposed to the air, white tendons, and ligaments. She could see the tears in his muscles, from continuously lifting heavy weights, that hadn't quite healed yet. His skin was completely gone along with his hair.

"How about now? You dig the look? I'm really yoked up."

Elyse screamed.

13

Distant Connections

ELYSE'S PHONE BUZZED NEXT to Karmina's and Victoria's. The entire wicker basket vibrated, and a name flashed across the screen. Skylar Babe with a heart emoji, a purple arrow passing through the heart's center. A soft tune emanated from the speaker, but no one was around to pick it up.

A plump jackrabbit sniffed the basket and hopped away.

On the other end of the phone was Skylar. This was the third time he tried calling Elyse in a two-hour period. She didn't respond to his texts, just checking up on her and the paranoia in his gut was nagging at him.

Something was wrong. He knew it. Elyse *always* got back to him within that timeframe.

Skylar grabbed a baseball bat, his brass knuckles his grandfather gifted him, and his car keys. He hopped inside his Jeep and threw on Travis Scott and started the car. Backing out of the driveway, he put the address in his GPS, and pulled off, tires screeching as he sped down the road.

Time to save my girl.

14

Soiled Masques Line the Walls

C OUGHING INTO HER fist, Victoria struggled to get off the ground. She felt like she fell five stories beneath the earth and her back ached in a hundred different places. It was as if a blind chiropractor put his hands on her back and did the worst job imaginable.

Victoria gagged, wishing she could plug her nostrils up with tissue. The overwhelming smell inside the rabbit hole was wretched and disgusting. It reminded her of a farm with wet feces and spoiled food cooking in the sun.

Rolling over, her itchy eyes began adjusting to the darkness and the dirt-packed walls became crystal clear. The light from above spilled down in weird ways, illuminating small bunnies all around her. Baby bunnies hopping to and fro.

They're so freaking adorable.

Victoria wished Elyse was here because she'd truly enjoy the moment and appreciate her sincerity. It almost made Victoria scoop one up and take it home—that is if she were to survive the night. Pushing the negative thoughts aside, she reached out and gently petted a baby bunny who seemed to relish the attention, pink nose turned upward.

Something rather large shifted in the darkness and sucking sounds followed. With the limited amount of light, Victoria discerned a massive furry hide, and maybe 11-15 bunnies crowded under the mystery animal. She moved closer, crouching down, not making any sudden movements. The sucking sounds grew louder and more desperate like this was giving the bunnies life.

Eww, nasty…

The bunnies were drinking milk, the stench hit her in a wave. And she assumed the massive shape shrouded in darkness had to be the mother. Nothing else made sense. The only problem was Victoria had never seen a bunny this fucking big before. It looked like it was the size of a rhinoceros. She slowly backed away, being careful not to make too much noise. Something in her gut twisted and turned, telling her to get away. She remembered how protective mothers are over their children and bunnies were no different. She didn't want to find out what this giant bunny mother was capable of in an enraged state.

Victoria looked up towards the light, trying to figure out how she can climb out of this damn hell hole. She experimented with indoor and outdoor rock climbing a couple of times with a few of her cousins, but she hated the experience. It was too sweaty and she was worried it was going to make her look too masculine over time with extreme definition in her muscles and she didn't want that. Plus, she hated how her cousins called her a gumby; she much rather be called a newbie than that dumb shit. Pulling on the knowledge from these limited sessions, she searched for a grip in the wall and found a small one, followed by a flat rock jutting out of the dirt a few feet above.

Grunting, she pulled herself up, back muscles screaming in pain. She ignored the agony in her back and searched for the next indentation. Her sweat-drenched hair clung to her skin like a jellyfish, an itch begging to be scratched, and she slid her hand into a dark crevice, gaining leverage. Her other hand fumbled around for something to grip. A round rock would have to do, there wasn't any other choice. She had to make do with what the rabbit hole had to offer.

Moving upward, she searched for somewhere to rest her hand and her right foot slipped, tread struggling to find traction against the flat surface.

Oh no, no, no, no, no. Please don't slip. Not now. Not now. Not—

Victoria slipped, hands scraping against the dirt face as she slid back down, sloppily landing on the ground on her side. Her hearing went funny and her right arm buzzed with pain, bones feeling like they were humming a tender tune. Something squealed underneath her, struggling to escape the weight of her. She rolled over and one of the bunnies seemed to be in bad shape, hopping with a limp, its small body smushed down. One eye dangled out the socket and blood soaked its furry coat.

This is bad news. There's no way the mother didn't hear that squeal.

An adrenaline spike helped Victoria get back up, the pain a dim memory. She expected the bunny mother to come charging, but nothing happened. That's when a sharp sound cut through the darkness—a harsh grinding. A grinding of small bunny teeth. It was impossible to ignore and seemed to send a message throughout the fluffle. The baby bunnies seemed agitated, hopping more erratically.

The bunny mother poked its head out of the darkness, fur caked with several layers of dirt. It seemed old and wizened as if it had been down here giving birth to bunnies for centuries. Thick shadows cut through its face, and Victoria struggled to discern its true countenance. When it came closer, the mother seemed to be wearing a dirt mask of sorts.

"Adorn the mask, child."

Victoria thought she was losing her mind. Did the mother just speak?

"Excuse, me?"

"You heard me. Adorn the mask. It's either that or I kill you for hurting my offspring."

"O-okay, whatever you say."

Victoria approached the mother with the utmost caution and reached her hands out. The wet dirt rippled and a clay mask plopped out of the soil. She grabbed it and hated the consistency. Part of her considered saying fuck it, throwing the mask, and making a run for it, but she had no idea how deep this rabbit hole went. What if she got lost? And she was sure the mother knew the environment much better than she did. Going against her better judgment, Victoria adorned the mask, nearly going blind. She blinked and her eyes adjusted to holes that seemed to adjust to her eyes. The clay sank into her pores, and rooted more deeply into her face. She attempted to pull it off, but it was stuck. She could breathe, but this seemed like a foul trick.

Don't trust the bunnies.

Stephanie's sweet voice flooded through Victoria's head and she freaked out. She struggled to speak, her lips feeling as if they had been stitched shut. Sweat dripped down her neck, spilling down from the crevices between her face and the mask.

"Calm down, child. This is part of the ceremony."

Calm down? How the fuck do I calm down?

Victoria took a deep breath, waiting for instructions and the distinct possibility of her body giving out from stress and mental exhaustion.

"You've worn masks for too long, this mask will absorb these guises, and you will face your face as it truly is. Feel your pain and allow the healing to begin. You will come out of this a woman, proud of your own skin, your own heart, and will no longer need these masques that have served you for so long."

Victoria shook her head, muffled words leaked out whatever this thing was that she deemed an ill-fitting description of a mouth. She didn't want this to happen, she didn't want to let go of her masks. She didn't know what life looked like without the safety of their touch, the protection of the emotional veils. Life would never be the same and Victoria was far ready for the immensity of this type of change in her day to day.

"Stop fighting the tide, child. It's too late to change what has already transpired."

Raging against the mask and the words, Victoria staggered around the rabbit hole. Her face tingled and her body felt as if valves were being opened up at various emotional points. Mental and emotional pain rose to the surface of Victoria's awareness like a horrid gas. Traumatic memories flashed before her eyes and a deep emotional pain racked her body. She collapsed to her knees, cradling her clay head in her hands, and mud seeped down her neck, plopping on the floor.

Behind her mask, hot tears saturated her face and her makeup was a thing of the past. Victoria attempted to pull the mask off a second time, desperately wanting the pain to stop, the memories to drip away, but the mask remained firmly fitted and wasn't moving a damn inch.

Just when Victoria thought she was becoming accustomed to the pain and gaining some sort of foothold in her emotional hell, a second wave of pain hit her and the sound of her old masks cracking filled her ears. The unpleasant sound grew in volume until her ears rang and the sound became a torrential death march with drums that wouldn't stop banging and a sinister rhythm that made her heart skip a beat.

She just prayed that someone could hear her above the sinister din.

15

Rathke's Dispatch

Deputy Alexander Rathke had his feet kicked up on the dashboard as he sipped on Big Gulp, condensation coating the plastic like a wet sleeve. Green Day's album *Nimrod* spilled out the speakers as Rathke scrolled down his Facebook feed on his phone. He bit on the straw and almost spilled his drink when dispatch screeched.

He grabbed the Motorola radio and pressed a button on the side. "Go ahead."

"Rathke, I need you to investigate the Kusama farm. Noise complaints. Probably some dumbass kids getting drunk and rowdy."

Rathke sighed dramatically and took another sip from his drink, biting on the straw. He could taste the high fructose corn syrup coating the back of his throat and ignored the mucus beginning to form back there.

"I'm on it, Janice."

He'd been sitting on this dirt road sheathed in darkness, for a few hours, listening to the crickets chirp and a random plane flying overhead. Supposed to be catching speeding cars, but he'd already reached his quota for the month, and he desired some solitude. Living in Plainfield his entire 42 years made him wince at all the changes the village experienced. He didn't do well with change. He wished for things to go back to the old days. There was a time there weren't so many damn kids, and don't even get him started on the newfound diversity hires in the police department.

Plumes of thick dust rose in the air as Rathke backed up the car. He turned up the volume, bobbing his head to the drums, and headed towards Kusama farm. He'd met Yayoi a couple decades ago and she was as kooky as a bat but easy on the eyes. Everyone knew her estranged granddaughter Stephanie stayed on the property. She too was gorgeous, but she said things that made Alexander's skin crawl and the crowns on his teeth ache. Blasphemous things that made him unconsciously grip his Glock 22 service pistol with his right hand just to make sure it was still there.

He cruised down the road, knowing the route by heart. These roads were imprinted in his mind like a worn map.

He prided himself on not needing to rely on technology like the younger generation. The horizon stretched out in front of him, the glare on his windshield twisting the flat landscape into a fiery panorama that crackled in the distance.

16

Helicopters Pass in the Dark of Night

T HE SMALL CANOE ROCKED back and forth, water splashing Karmina. She closed her eyes, gripping the oars for dear life, afraid they would slip from her hands. Something swam underneath the boat and she wondered if it was a shark or some other underwater creature that was disturbed by her presence. She even thought about the creature in the rabbit holes from earlier, maybe it followed her into the portal, wanting to finish the job.

Something fleshy shot out of the water and gripped the side of the boat. Fingers sank into the yam-like material, finding purchase.

Karmina watched in terror as she saw another hand shoot out of the water, finding leverage, pulling itself out of the milky depths. Petrified, she felt dumb for waiting so long to come to her senses. She didn't want to be the first girl killed off in one of those horror flicks, the helpless one who did nothing to fight off the monster. Hating the possibility of herself becoming that horror trope, she gripped the oar and swung at the thing pulling itself over the side. The oar's edge smacked the side of the thing's head and it fell unconscious with a soft groan. She pushed the pale thing that resembled a man over, and she gasped when she saw it resembled Oswaldo with his cleft chin, tell-tale mustache, and lively eyes. The only difference was its skin seemed bulbous and yam-like. Barnacles decorated his chest, legs, and wrist like subaquatic body jewelry.

Maybe this was *him*, she reasoned. Maybe this was her brother and he stumbled across another rendition of the Frolicking some time ago and got stuck inside the portal. He obviously needed saving, but how did he know she was outside the portal? She couldn't see outside, let alone hear what was taking place outside of these walls no matter how hard she wished she could.

Karmina lightly smacked his cheek, hoping it would wake him up. He groaned and snatched her hand, applying pressure to the eight small bones in her wrist.

"Oswaldo, please stop!" Karmina said, feeling the pain intensify by the second. "Don't break my fucking wrist."

"Say helicopters pass in the dark of night three times and I'll let go."

"Please…"

"Say it!"

Karmina said it as quickly as possible and Oswaldo made good on his word, instantly letting go of her hand. She massaged her wrist, almost not believing this moment was real, but the pain told her this very much was real and reminded her that her brother had almost broken her wrist. He was the same bully from her childhood, just a grown one.

Karmina looked at his mottled flesh and wondered if her brother was rotting to death or if the water had infected him past the point of no return.

He sat up, lunging forward and bear-hugged her, reeking of saltwater and mildew.

"I missed you so much! You have no idea," he said.

"I'm having a hard time breathing."

"Just giving you some brotherly love," he said, letting go at the last minute.

"Save that shit for someone else," Karmina said through labored breaths. She could have sworn he wanted her to feel more pain than usual.

Oswaldo snorted and scoffed, spitting a phlegm over the side of the boat.

"Where's everyone else?" Karmina asked, regaining her composure. "I heard their voices inside the living room."

"Ah this place works differently," he said, pointing to the yam-like plants hanging out of the walls, coated in a bland white paint. They moved with a liveliness though, white birds perched on the branches. "Your brothers are everywhere."

"I want to see them though, with my own eyes."

"You sure?"

"Yeah, I'm sure."

Oswaldo gripped his chest, ripping his pectorals open, with with a sickening tear. No blood or fluids spilled out. Instead, dried flecks of paint flew into the air like dust and Karmina coughed, wondering if this was going to impact her health in the long run.

Three small familiar heads attached to a stalk swirled out of his chest, the heads growing larger in size, sleepy eyes blinking open. Fear gripped Karmina's heart and she thought back to her bad shroom trip, feeling that dread creep up.

She backed up, careful not to go over the edge of the boat.

"What's wrong, sis?" Yandel asked, the biggest head growing from the stalk. "I thought you missed us."

Efrain spoke up in his gritty voice, "Guess she doesn't. Might have to put hands on her. Teach her a lesson."

Karmina grabbed an oar and swung it at Oswaldo's neck. He ducked down, air ruffling his wet black hair.

"Almost got me, sis. Next time, have better aim."

"How's this for better aim?"

She jammed the oar inside his chest with a furious speed, cutting off one of the heads. The oar lodged itself inside Oswaldo's chest.

"That's fucked up, Mina," Raul said. "You killed Yandel. You killed your own blood."

"You're no blood of mine. You're a bunch of *babosos*. Something out of a nightmare used to fuck with my head."

"I think we might have to hurt you," Efrain said. "Bet you'll make a tasty *chamberete*."

Karmina grabbed the other oar, keeping the creature posing as her brothers at a distance. The canoe lazily floated along the white river. Her brothers sat there, staring at her, not once blinking their eyes.

The walls around Karmina teemed with life: flora and fauna, jade plants, avocados, Mexican mints, and mahogany shook in and out of the paint. Something about the biodiverse reminded her of home, but she was still on alert, forcing her eyes to stay on Oswaldo, examining his body language for his next move.

The thing lunged forward and Karmina swung the oar, connecting with its head. The oar broke in half, one end soaring into the water, the other held in her hand like a spear. She stared down at the sharp piece, astounded that she was getting the best of her brothers.

Oswaldo snorted and spat out blood, spittle coating the bottom of the boat. "I'm going to fuck you up for that."

The other brothers mumbled amongst themselves, cursing her. Karmina crouched down in a defensive posture, ready for their next move. Oswaldo lunged forward and Karmina impaled him with the broken oar, blood bubbling in his neck. The weight of his body pushed her back and she plunged down into the lukewarm water. The consistency was thick as syrup, but seemed light at the same time.

She didn't realize how deep she had fallen into the water until she swam and swam and swam upward. Finally, she broke through the water's surface and threw an arm over the side of the canoe. Her body ached from the effort, but she managed to pull herself over. She huffed and puffed, slowly gaining her breath. Her brothers were gone.

Karmina felt something rising from her chest. She coughed, smiled and then laughed. She laughed a laugh so freeing, she almost couldn't believe it. Thought she was losing her mind, but she didn't care. Something about this was liberating.

Something fizzled and crackled, a black dot opened in front of Karmina and she laughed her way through the other side, barely being able to breathe, sides cramping from laughter.

17

Running Suicides

ELYSE SPRINTED THROUGH THE mirrored rooms, lungs on fire. She heard the heavy footfalls of her boyfriend or what she assumed was her boyfriend, gaining on her. Horror and desperate reflections surrounded her as she caught glimpses of herself, skin shining with sweat, eyes wide as a deer's caught in the headlights of an obnoxious driver, high beams turned to the max.

She was a decent runner and even participated in various running clubs throughout the years, but these rooms seemed to stretch into infinity. Mirrors and mirrored objects everywhere. If this was an exhibit or a museum, Elyse would have adored it and found beauty in the space. However, being chased and running for her life, turned this into a hellish obstacle course. She took sharp pivots and hopped over weird shapes, the entire time seeing her face everywhere she turned.

Someone once told her to never look back when running a race, that you would slow down, lose your footing or even your pace. She kept a consistent rhythm, determined to find the portal's exit, but nothing was changing. There were no signs of the black dot, no dots whatsoever outside of the weird colorful ones floating in the air. She smacked a few, that felt soft and squishy, but they would always return to their original positioning like a prearranged map of stars in a universe forged from pure chaos.

Her brain searched for a solution, analyzing every angle. That's when she remembered the bear mace. She didn't want to hurt anyone and she had no choice but to use a weapon at this point. She had her back against the proverbial wall or in this case, mirror. Fishing the bear mace out of her swinging tote bag managed to be much more difficult than she could imagine as she continued running.

Her left side was beginning to cramp and what masqueraded as her boyfriend was getting closer with no signs of letting up. She could almost feel his hot breath on her shoulders and ears. Dipping to the right, she cut into another room, readying her finger on the spray's trigger.

He came around the corner with bloodshot eyes, muscles tensed and ready to pounce on her.

"Tsavad tanem," he said, grinning maniacally.

Let me take your pain away…

Elyse's body tensed, knowing he meant every word, feeling death buzzing in his head. She hated the fact that this place was fucking with her like this, preying on her fears. Stephanie said this was supposed to be a transformative experience, but it turned out to be nothing short of a nightmare. She waited a few heart beats until he was close enough and she sprayed it directly into his eyes. The scream he let out sounded otherworldly and animalistic. She kicked his exposed balls and sprayed him one more time for good measure. His hands were covering his eyes while a gooey white substance spilled down his cheeks, seeping out from under his palms. Vitreous humor, collagen, and a dash of blood coating his face like makeup.

Elyse continued running, somehow finding a second wind. A black dot loomed in the distance and she knew this was her chance. The man who pretended to be her boyfriend continued screaming a guttural cry and weeping in the same breath. She heard him say something about his eyes over and over.

She hopped out of the portal and landed back in the grassy field, landing on her side. The landing wasn't too bad, but it was so dark outside. Relieved to be alive, Elyse wasn't quite sure what to do with herself. The portal closed and the screams stopped with it.

Wanting to get as far away from the portal as possible, she started running and tripped, sinking into the earth. It felt like a bomb had gone off in her ankle, and she looked down at a rabbit hole that seemed to consume her leg. She pulled on her leg, struggling to escape and screamed with exhaustion.

When will this night end?

18

Pumpkin Season

THE CAR DOOR WHINED like a dying horse as Deputy Rathke slowly got out of the police vehicle. He snorted and spat a wad of mucus on the asphalt. The night air had a slight chill so he grabbed a light jacket and he fished for his flashlight in the backseat. Clicking on the flashlight, he started making his way to the entrance of the Kusama farm.

It seemed somewhat peaceful, seeing the trees sway back and forth, but the darkness in the field was disconcerting. The flashlight cut out a small path in front of him as he stepped on a dead cornstalk underneath the weight of his worn boots.

"Jesus Christ, Stephanie. Lucky, I got on an old pair of boots." He struggled to wipe the smushed corn off his sole and sighed. His flashlight revealed a booth filled with alcohol lining the walls. The lines in his forehead furrowed as he remembered the sharp taste of whiskey that used to comfort him after his divorce from his wife. That was a rough time, a black hole that nearly swallowed him whole. He managed to climb back out, swearing off alcohol and getting sober. Part of him considered breaking the bottles in an assault against his past, but this wasn't his property and who knew if Stephanie had hidden cameras set up on the property in key locations.

Better to just move on.

A dog yapped in the distance and the flashlight went out. Rathke smacked the flashlight with his palm, cursing the object for not working properly.

Blasted flashlight. Need to replace the batteries when I get back.

The flashlight came back on, calming his overly caffeinated nerves. His nerves didn't stay calm for too long once he looked down as he saw mice swarming around his feet. He kicked one and it squealed. Moving off a wicked concoction of pure instinct and fear, Rathke pulled out his Glock 22 and let off two shots into the mice. They scurried off into the darkness and two small brown bodies laid at his feet, blood pooling beneath his boots.

After reholstering his Glock, Rathke wiped the sweat from his brow and continued moving through the cornfield, wondering if anyone heard the gunshots. The strange thing about it, he didn't hear any out-of-the-ordinary sounds since he'd been investigating the property. Maybe someone misheard something out here or maybe it was a prank call. He thought about turning around and heading back to the car when he heard a blood-curdling scream.

Rathke pulled his Glock back out and angled it forward while holding the flashlight out. He ran towards the sound, skirting around a weirdly structured set of haystacks. It looked like someone could get lost inside and he was thankful he didn't risk making that expedition. He moved into a grassy field, lungs on fire, another reminder that he needed a consistent workout schedule instead of Netflix binges at night.

"Hello!" he yelled, hoping someone would make a sound or some sort of clue as to the whereabouts of the victim who emitted the cry in the first place. "I'm here to help. It's the police."

He paused and didn't hear a sound. That's when he noticed black dots floating in the air. He would have rubbed his eyes if it wasn't for his hands being full.

Must be seeing things…

The dots grew larger as he cautiously approached one. It called him, not verbally, but energetically, nudging him forward. It felt like home in a sense even though he had no idea what the hell he was looking at. He almost put his gun away, but he forced it to stay in his hand as he entered the portal.

Inside the portal, Rathke was faced with a number of pumpkins with strange dots lining the outside. Part of his mind, struggled to make sense of what was going on. Something felt off about all of this so he grabbed the radio off his shoulder and called dispatch.

"Dispatch, this is Deputy Rathke, come in. I need backup at the Kusama farm."

The radio hissed and sputtered, the frequency turning into white noise at the other end. He tried it two more times, getting the same result.

Fuck.

He turned off the flashlight since there was plenty of sunlight coming down from the sky. His head hurt, trying to rationalize the sudden shift from night to day. He considered turning around and leaving, but his sense of duty caused him to stay put and explore the space.

Rathke weaved his way between the massive pumpkins, enjoying the sweet smell of the ground vegetables. He thought about taking one back home, but he didn't quite know if they were safe to eat with the strange polka dots decorating the outside. Something about them seemed poisonous or toxic.

He heard a noise in the distance and ran towards it. Skirting around a corner, he tumbled into a black hole. His body felt as if it had gone through a light hangover and his mouth felt dry as the desert. Aching, he slowly stood and looked around his surroundings. It was pretty dark, but he managed to find his flashlight along with his Glock 22. He clicked the flashlight back on and a swath of light cut through the foul darkness, revealing a fluffle of bunnies hopping on the ground. Part of him gagged, smelling shit in the air. He wasn't sure how he didn't notice it the moment he became conscious again.

Someone groaned and Rathke spun towards the sound, shining his light on some monstrous being with an execrable face. It looked like hardened clay with twigs and rocks embedded in the texture. The thing had a body similar to a woman's, but it was coated in dirt and grime. Its mouth struggled to open, wet strings of soil stretching between lips that hadn't seen the light of day in ages. A centipede crawled out of its cheek, squirming up the face and disappearing into its long hair.

A slender hand outstretched towards Rathke and a feminine screech escaped its throat. Startling Rathke, he quickly upped his Glock and pulled the trigger twice. Two shots punctured the face and the mask cracked into pieces, slowly sinking down to the floor, revealing a young woman's pretty face, skin glowing. She collapsed to the floor.

Rathke ran up to the woman, realizing that he may have committed murder and jail had to be in his future.

"I–I'm sorry," he said, barely containing himself. He was on the verge of blabbering and sobbing. "I was scared. I didn't know."

Something made the space around him shake and he shone the light into the darkness, exposing a gargantuan bunny. It snorted, making Rathke gag as the fetid odor washed over him. He stood on shaky feet and staggered backward. Rathke upped his gun once again, letting off ten rounds into the beast. It screamed at such a high pitch, it made Rathke piss himself, the warm remnants of his Big Gulp spilling down his leg.

Moving back, Rathke looked behind him and noticed the black dot from earlier ripping into the space, calling his name once again. Hope rippled through Rathke's chest as he slowly stepped towards it. The portal exit seemed so close yet so far away.

The bunny mother moved forward, blood blinding its black eyes, but it could smell Rathke's sweat and fearful pheromones permeating throughout the space.

Rathke thought he was losing his mind inside this rabbit hole and wondered if his sanity had slipped away somewhere on the drive over to the Kusuma farm. He knew there was something cursed when it came to that namesake and that bloodline. The damn grandma voluntarily lived inside an insane asylum despite making tons of money off her art.

Eyeing the black dot behind him, Rathke crept towards the portal while keeping his gun aimed at the bunny. He let off the last three remaining bullets and ejected the chamber. Searching his tactical duty belt, he couldn't find his extra magazine, figuring it must have slipped out during the fall.

Rathke was inches away from leaving this hellhole, when the bunny mother bit into his soft stomach, tearing away the flesh, and coming away with a length of intestines. His free hand punched through the portal, followed by a portion of his arm. He tried to force himself away from the bunny, but a hot pain flashed through his entire body and blood gushed out the hole in his gut. The black dot decreased in size and his arm felt as if an anaconda had wrapped itself around his arm. He pulled on it, but it was stuck. Before the pain grew to unbearable proportions, the bunny buried its face in his stomach, biting through his liver and puncturing one lung. The cascading pain overwhelmed Rathke and he passed out.

19

The Fruit of Authenticity

VICTORIA TOUCHED HER FACE, barely believing her luck, somehow she was still alive. There were no signs of any damage done to her skin. The clay mask had absorbed the full impact of the shots and simply knocked her off her feet. The shock caused her to swim into a dark pool of blackness and when she got up, the cop seemed to be gone.

Did I hallucinate the man in a state of delirium?

Her question was answered when she heard the bunny mother snoring as she slept soundly in the darkness, the outline of her furry body rising and falling with each breath. That's when Victoria noticed the slick pool of blood and the remains of the cop sticking out of the darkness. Part of her felt horrified at what happened, while another part of her took a sick satisfaction at the sight of his mangled body. The latter part seemed to spread outward, and she embraced it.

Bastard had it coming to him.

She walked as if she were in a lucid dream, noticing the lack of weight and pressure on her shoulders. It was weird feeling this way because there was a sense of airiness to her demeanor, a sense of newfound freedom and joy blooming in her chest. Maybe there was something to this frolicking stuff. She didn't have to hide her true self anymore, she could authentically be Victoria with no reservations. It was time for the world and her friends to witness her in her entirety for the first time.

Something crackled behind her and the black portal exit loomed in front of Victoria. It seemed like it was time to go so she calmly stepped out and found herself back in the grassy field. She took a deep inhale, ready to grab the world by the balls and twist it to the left.

Victoria hummed to herself as she made her way to the house. She was going to get her phone back one way or another. Before trying the back door, she slipped out of her pants, crouched down and took a piss in the grass, relishing the sound of her bladder being emptied. She didn't bother wiping, threw the pants back on and found the back door conveniently unlocked, and she slipped her way inside. She openly explored the house, moving from room to room. It wasn't anything special and this disappointed Victoria since she expected the place to give

some insight into the inner world of that crazy bitch
Stephanie.

The wicker basket sat on Stephanie's king-sized
California bed. Victoria scooped her phone up and
shoved it into her pocket. She grabbed the other
phones, tossed them on the floor and stomped on
them, putting her full weight onto the devices. Bitches
should have listened to her when she gave them a
chance. Why should they hand over their phones to
a complete stranger? It was ludicrous behavior and she
didn't fully understand why she gave into the peer
pressure.

Victoria brushed it off, stopping herself from
scolding herself. That was the old her, that Victoria
died in the rabbit hole and was slowly decomposing.
This was the real Victoria, the one that had be
desperate to come to the forefront for her entire life.
It was so refreshing to be herself.

She found a raggedy stuffed bunny on the bed and
punched in the face and gut repeatedly. The stitching
around the stomach ripped apart and Victoria pulled
out tufts of cotton, tossing them in the air.

How fun.

Giving into her impulses was fun, it felt *right*. She
vowed to never go against herself again.

Victoria thought about finding the girls, but she said
fuck it. She yawned and looked at the time on her phone-

3:22 am. *Jesus Christ, it's late. Think it's time to go home. Those cunts could die out here for all I care.*

Victoria made her way back out the house, and heard a commotion inside. She thought about turning back to investigate, but she shrugged and thought to herself, *not my business.*

The night seemed to be beautiful and the moon beamed down at her with a sickly radiance. She enjoyed the light and skipped her way through the field until she noticed Elyse in distress.

"Victoria, please help me!" Elyse pleaded. "I'm stuck."

"How did this happen?" Victoria said, crouching down.

"I-I don't know. I was running and tripped in a rabbit hole. Help me. Please!"

"Hmmmmm…" Victoria said, tapping her index finger on her lips. "Should have been more careful."

"Why are you acting like this?" Elyse asked. "What the fuck is wrong with everyone? You're my friend, you're supposed to help."

"I pretended to be your friend, you dense cunt," Victoria said. "Hopefully, it's a sprained ankle and not a broken foot."

"C'mon Victoria, don't be like this."

"I'm just being myself. My true self. Goodbye, Elyse."

"I can't believe you, you fake bitch. I thought you were better than this."

"Spoiler alert—I'm not."

Victoria walked away, tuning out the curses Elyse verbally threw her way. None of them affected her in the slightest and she didn't feel one ounce of empathy for her former friend. She hoped the bitch would rot out here for all she cared. Returning to skipping at a light pace, she found herself back in the parking lot and pulled out her keys. She noticed the cop car and scoffed, remembering his pointed gun and fucked up body.

After typing her address into the phone, she slid into the driver's seat and noticed things felt ten times better without the girls. Having the car to herself was pleasant and she felt like she could breathe.

She switched on her headlights, which cut through the darkness like blades, and she revved the engine. Backing her car out of the spot, she sped out of the parking lot and hopped back on the road.

"Sayanora, bitches," she yelled as she flicked off the Kusuma farm with her free hand.

20

Family History & Elder Dumplings

BLOOD TRAILED DOWN THE steps leading up to the old home and the front door was cracked open, screen door slamming with each gust of wind. Karmina went inside, careful not to disturb anything. It seemed normal enough, a small foyer in the front with minimal furniture. Shoes lined a brown shelf in front of what Karmina assumed to be a coat closet. She wondered if Victoria or Elyse had been hurt.

The living room was sparse with some weird lights, a few blankets carefully folded on a yellow couch with a flat-screen TV mounted on a wall. A purple light glowed behind it.

There was a slight thud in the next room adjacent to the living room and a groan. Karmina carefully made her way over, wishing she had a gun in hand or something just as deadly. With hushed breath, Karmina shuffled into the kitchen, expecting something crazy like one of her brothers to pop out, but it seemed normal minus the body slouched next to the fridge on the floor.

"Hi, Karmina," said Stephanie with a slurred voice. "Welcome to mi casa. Home sweet home."

"What the fuck happened to you?" Karmina said, shocked. She never expected to see their host in a weakened state. "Are you okay?"

Stephanie still looked beautiful, but her dress had tears and gashes through it as if she had gotten into a fight with a rhinoceros and somehow won to tell the tale. She had scratches and nicks all over her skin. However, the biggest wound was on her calf, blood pooling around her form. Stephanie slowly wrapped gauze around the wound. A bottle of hydrogen peroxide sat next to her, the smell thick in the stuffy kitchen air.

"I'm okay."

Karmina bent down, looking into wild eyes of Stephanie. She felt concern and worry for the girl. Maybe she should call the cops or an ambulance or both.

"What happened? This looks pretty serious."

"Parts of me were obliterated, the parts that were no longer necessary. The parts that no longer served me. That's part of this experience, the design."

"I'm sorry, but I don't understand at all."

"Let me tell you a story to illustrate my point...once upon a time, when I was a teenager, somewhere around 14 or 15, my grandma Yayoi kept me up late at night. It was on Easter. She looked down at me with a solemn face, dried paint smeared across her cheeks and neck and said get up. I received a cute Easter basket and she fed me strange chocolates along with a bitter-tasting tea. She took me outside, holding my hand as dark dots floated around her head like a charred halo. She reassured me this was normal. Dots followed her."

"She taught me how to frolic, skipping through the field together hand in hand. Colorful dots appeared in the field. Cerulean blue, lavender and a mucus yellow. I chose the lavender one and grandma helped me climb inside."

"I'm not sure why grandma left me alone since she usually looked after me, but I wasn't scared in the slightest. It was a plain white room at first glance...colorful dots bled through the walls, the floor, and the ceiling. I don't know how to explain it; but they seemed to have a foreign consciousness, a hyper intelligence. They bled through these surfaces, taking physical shape. The dots multiplied at a rapid volume and intensity. They tickled at first when they touched my skin, but they began to enter my body. Feeling something like bubbles, I laughed, but my laughter turned into a dreadful confusion. They touched the weak parts of me, the ugly parts I shoved away; but they saw everything. They brought these parts to the surface, spinning in strange patterns, obliterating the fluff and reintegrating the rest into my being."

"I cried and cried, purging years of buried trauma," Stephanie sniffled and wiped away a tear. "At some point, I passed out and I woke with my grandma at my side. She caressed my forehead, humming a soothing tune both mournful and uplifting. She took my hand and we walked out of the portal. I was reborn in a bed of obliteration."

"Wow, that's pretty incredible, but what about your leg?" Karmina said. "Aren't you concerned about it healing properly? We should probably get you to a hospital."

"I appreciate your concern, makes me feel touched, but I'll be fine," Stephanie said. "The night is almost over and we have one last thing to accomplish."

Karmina sighed, hoping the kind gesture would help Stephanie, but also get their phones back in hand. She wondered if they would ever get them back.

"Help me stand up, please," Stephanie extended her hands to the air like a child needing support.

Karmina took the girl's damp hands in her own and with considerable effort, pulled her to her feet. Something drew Karmina's attention to the photos, newspaper clipping, and magazine stories clamped to the fridge door with Easter themed magnets. One said "Priestess of Polka

Dots: Yayoi Kusama" while another said "The Return of Kusama." One photo was of an older woman, with sharp features, vibrantly dyed red hair, and a red polka dot dress. Another one was the same woman, but several decades younger, black hair, red body suit, hands situated behind her head. This one reminded her of Stephanie, they shared similar features.

"Who is this?" Karmina asked, curious, yet assuming it had to be the pop artist family member.

"My grandma Yayoi, she's my elder dumpling. Wish she would come visit more often."

The pained look on Stephanie's face resembled her own when she thought back to her family. Karmina pulled Stephanie in and gave her a warm hug.

"Thank you. I needed that."

"So, about this feast?"

21

Easter Supper

ELYSE TOOK ABOUT 20 minutes to free herself from the clutches of the rabbit hole. She'd never broken a bone in her life so she didn't know what to medically call what happened to her. She didn't hear anything break, but she couldn't be sure. She limped forward with each stride, a hot burst of pain bubbling up her ankle every time, shooting up her leg.

That conniving snake, Victoria. I should have known better.

The signs were there the entire time. Her intuition told her and even Skylar mentioned something about her character after meeting her the first time.

Elyse adjusted her tote bag on her shoulder and headed back in the direction of the cars. She remembered hearing the rev of the engine and feeling the sharp pangs of betrayal cut into her heart. Victoria wasn't the best friend ever, but she never thought she would stoop to this level and leave Karmina and her stranded. She was hoping Stephanie would keep her words so she could call her boyfriend to pick them up or order them a ride home.

She found Karmina and Stephanie sitting at a large wooden table. Several chairs surrounded it and stuffed animals sat in each seat, a plate and cutlery for each one. Elyse took a moment and rubbed her eyes since she wasn't sure if her sense of reality was becoming completely unmoored the further the night progressed.

"Elyse, I'm so happy you made it!" Stephanie cheered. "Come sit down, we've been waiting."

Elyse limped towards an empty seat facing Karmina who looked like she survived one of the roughest gauntlets known to man. Her friend looked cold-faced and wasn't giving her any hint as to what was going on.

"What happened to your leg?" Stephanie asked, shock and concern painting her face. "You need some help."

"Tripped over a rabbit hole, think I sprained my ankle. Not sure."

"Told you to be careful of those rabbits. Hope you're okay though."

"I'll survive."

"If it's any consolation, my leg got fucked up too," Stephanie stood, pulling one leg up that had gauze wrapped around it in several layers, blood seeping out the bottom.

"We're trauma twins!"

Elyse nodded, not having the energy to entertain this girl much longer. She just wanted to go home, and go to sleep in the comfort of her own bed.

"Have a seat!" Stephanie said. "This is a celebratory feast. Important to regain your energy and those valuable nutrients you lost during your experiences. I took the liberty of making a variety of dishes and I have vegan options as well."

Stephanie winked and Karmina seemed to be on the brink of having a breakdown or killing everyone. Either way, Elyse felt like their night was coming to an end and maybe it was time for an escape, but to where? They were so far from the actual village and it could take hours before they would reach someone who could help.

Stephanie's eye twitched while she passed around steamed plates of food that made Elyse's stomach grumble. She was surprised by her own hunger after everything she witnessed. Placing steamed vegetables, and other items on her plate, she was looking forward to the food. Still, she was concerned about Karmina who seemed to be signaling something with her eyes, but Elyse couldn't make it out.

What are you trying to tell me?

Stephanie turned to the stuffed bunny with floppy ears, a tuxedo, and a top hat. She grabbed it by the neck, took her steak knife, and stabbed it repeatedly. Thick red tufts of cotton spilled out.

"Let this motherfucker be an example," Stephanie said, standing up and dangling the stuffed animal by its ears. "He thought he could leave the table without being excused. He thought he could leave the property before we finished celebrating. It looks like Mr. Fancy Pants thought wrong."

Karmina's eyes pleaded with Elyse. Elyse's heart ached and she realized something deeply wrong was occurring. Stephanie broke out into laughter as she bit into a large turkey leg. She chewed with her mouth open and downed it with some water.

It was beginning to be too much for Elyse and tears rose to the surface as she felt trapped in this scenario. She wished her boyfriend was here or there was a way to leave, but she knew it was too risky. The tears intensified and Elyse sniffled, mucus dribbling down her lips. This wasn't what Easter was about, this was something else entirely and it was getting to her.

"Why am I still alive?" Elyse asked, shocked by her own question, tears running down her dirt-stained cheeks. She never thought about wanting to die so early in life, but tonight had taken a toll on her from all angles. "Just kill me please."

"Because you respect this sacred holiday, unlike your *friends*. I don't even know how you get along with them.

I mean you have decorum and the pure joy of Easter emanating off you like a young child. I would never dispose of someone like that. Don't you understand?"

Elyse shook her head. "Why do you continue hurting me?"

"For fun, silly," Stephanie said, grinning. Her gap-toothed smile made Elyse shiver.

The sound of a car swerving outside interrupted their interaction and Elyse felt a pang of hope rising in her chest. Maybe the cops knew something terribly wrong had happened and came to investigate with a SWAT team in tow. The sheer weight of the situation lifted, and hope bubbled in Elyse's rapidly beating heart.

"Fucking pigs," Stephanie said, gritting her teeth. "I hate the cops."

Stephanie clapped her hands twice and a mutant bunny shook the sleep from its pitch-black eyes and slowly rose to its feet, hopping out of a chair, awaiting further instructions.

"Maximoto, go see what that noise is, but be careful."

The bunny mutant nodded, thick strings of saliva dripped from the corners of its mouth and ran down its matted fur. Elyse didn't know how she never noticed the jackrabbit. For some reason, it blended in amongst the stuffed animals.

"Feel free to feed on anyone trying to disturb our meal."

The jackrabbit bent down, rippling muscles tensing, and ran on all fours at a frightening speed. Elyse felt sorry for whoever dared to come on the property. She silently prayed they brought weaponry or the very least a large team of people. Otherwise, it would be like cattle going to the slaughterhouse.

"Did you call someone?" Stephanie asked, leaning across the table.

"No, you took my phone," Elyse glared at Stephanie. "Remember?"

"Oh I forgot," Stephanie rubbed her head. "Sorry about that. You can always get another one when this is all over."

When this is all over? Was Stephanie planning on letting me live after this shitshow and all the carnage she subjected me to. Or was this a trick?

Elyse wasn't sure if she should get her hopes up or be grimly realistic. Either way, she was exhausted and all she wanted to do was curl up in her boyfriend's arms and go to sleep. Maybe she should have listened to him and brought a gun, but she doubted that was a good idea since she would probably put it to her own head just about now.

"Hey, stop frowning," Stephanie said, breaking Elyse's nihilistic train of thinking. "You should smile more. You're so pretty when you smile."

"I don't want to smile."

Stephanie leaned across the table and smacked Elyse across the face. "I said smile."

Elyse forced herself to smile, a hot searing pain spreading across her cheek. Karmina showed some emotion for the first time, empathy and concern pulling at her. Elyse disassociated from the present moment and imagined another reality where she and this schizo sitting across from her were best friends. Despite this vivid imagery, her smile wavered after a few minutes passed and hot tears ran down her face.

"That's better," Stephanie said, pleased with Elyse's forced display of happiness. "Both of you eat up. Don't want your food getting cold."

Elyse jammed her fork into a pile of spinach. Her appetite had disappeared after the violence, but she chewed, barely aware of the flavor. She swallowed the food and took another bite, staring into the heart of nothingness.

22

Antiquated Batting Cages

SKYLAR CRESCENT-MOONED THE WHIP into the parking lot, tires screeching on the asphalt, the world beyond the windshield a monochromatic blur of street lamps and inky black night. He felt blessed to have made it without getting pulled over.

When he noticed the cop car in the lot, it made him feel a sense of relief. Maybe the cops had been called and everything was being taken care of. Still, he didn't want to leave it to chance since he noticed Victoria's car was missing and no other cars were present. His intuition wasn't the best, but his gut wasn't at ease. Something was wrong.

Skylar dug into the backseat, searching for his bat. In the heat of things and rushing over here, he forgot his gun. He settled on the aluminum bat and felt more secure with the weight in his hand. He practiced swinging his bat at the moon, the grip of the handle digging into his palms.

Brass knuckles weighed down his right pocket, but he felt like the bat would be more than enough if anything were to go awry. He was prepared for whatever.

Through the darkness, Skylar noticed nearby shrubbery shaking. A muscular flash of white bounded towards him. Skylar took a batting stance and spit on the ground.

Looks like I'm up to bat…

Skylar swung at the man-sized jackrabbit, catching the beast in the shoulder. It yelped in pain, falling back to nurse its wound.

What the fuck? Am I dreaming or is this a giant rabbit?

These ruminations came to a quick end the moment the jackrabbit charged at Skylar, smacking him in the chest with its body weight. He rolled across the asphalt, small pieces of glass and sharp rocks cutting his exposed skin.

The massive jackrabbit hovered over Skylar, pinning him to the ground. Skylar shoved the bat under its neck, pushing against the jackrabbit's vicious attempts to bite his face off. Its teeth grinded against one another, sounding like knives sharpening knives. Skylar winced at the sound and kneed the jackrabbit's soft stomach. It screamed, falling to the side.

Skylar scrambled to his feet and wildly swung at the jackrabbit's head, connecting with a nasty *crunch*. Somehow the beast was still alive and managed to get back up so he swung again, breaking a leg and then another, crippling the jackrabbit. The screams pierced Skylar's ears, making him feel bad, but the adrenaline racing through his veins and his will to save his girl far outweighed any shred of empathy he had for the jackrabbit.

He slammed the bat down again and again, coating himself in geysers of blood. His arms ached with exhaustion and his lungs were on fire by the time he finished the deed.

23

The Compulsion

SOMETHING GOT INTO KARMINA—a burgeoning urge, a fervid compulsion to lose her shit. Little did she know, this was inner strength coming to the surface, a hidden part of her activated inside the portal. She swallowed down a forkful of mashed potatoes, barely registering the food and keeping her eyes on Stephanie and Elyse. Her heart ached for Elyse and she couldn't believe Stephanie slapped her a few minutes ago. She hated seeing her friend in distress and pain.

Karmina gripped the underside of the table, acrylic nails digging into the aged wood, and using all of her strength, flipped it on its side. Elyse and Stephanie let out cries of surprise and shock while gluttonous plates of food went flying. The beverages spilled and fluids splattered everywhere. Insects rushed to nibble on the chunks of food.

Stephanie fell on her back, momentarily dazed by Karmina's outburst.

Karmina rushed to Elyse's side, gripping her hand and forcefully pulling her up. "It's time for us to get the fuck out of here. C'mon!"

"O-okay," Elyse said, struggling to find her footing in the grass, pain shooting through her ankle.

Elyse did her best to keep up with Karmina, who pulled her along, jogging at a light pace. Karmina wanted to be gentler and take things slow, considering Elyse's injury, but they didn't have time. They had to get to the parking lot and meet whoever was out there. She just prayed they were still alive and that Maximoto hadn't killed the driver already.

Both Elyse and Karmina gasped when they saw Skylar covered in blood, trailing a steel bat behind him. Karmina wasn't sure if she was hallucinating or if this was a new threat that had spilled out of a portal. Tears of relief ran down Elyse's face as she ran up to her boyfriend, hugging him tightly despite the blood.

"I'm happy you're alive! I'm so sorry I didn't listen to you. This entire night has been a nightmare."

"It's okay, lovebug. Let's dip before any more bunny mutants try to kill us."

They slid into the car, not a single person bringing up the bloodied jackrabbit carcass laying in the parking lot. As Skylar backed the car up, they noticed Stephanie walk out, her dress a complete wreck, and screamed at the sight of Maximoto. The car moved onto the road and Karmina looked back and watched Stephanie cradle Maximoto's deformed head in her arms.

Skylar turned up the volume on the car's speakers to drown out the screams receding into the distance.

Acknowledgements

I want to give special thanks to Yayoi Kusama for helping serve as a creative catalyst for this book, Tierra Therese Ellis for being a beautiful muse, and helping me feel like I can do anything in this world, J. David Osborne for keeping me accountable with steady writing/word counts, Kelby Losack, David Simmons, and Eddy Rathke for their constant support and encouragement. I want to thank God, and the universe for assisting me in bringing this idea to life.

About the Author

Grant Wamack is the author of *Bullet Tooth, God's Leftovers, Black Gypsies, The Motorpapi Chronicles,* and *The Hum of the World & Other Stories.* He has more than 40 short stories published in places such as *Dark Moon Digest, The Best of Surreal Grotesque,* and *The New Flesh.* When he's not writing, he's reading tarot cards and practicing jiu jitsu in LA. You can follow his come-up over at his newsletter Literary Loud: https://grantwamack.substack.com/